THE MOVING FINGER

Agatha Christie®

The Moving Finger

HarperCollins*Publishers*

HarperCollins*Publishers*
1 London Bridge Street
London SE1 9GF
www.harpercollins.co.uk

HarperCollins*Publishers*
Macken House, 39/40 Mayor Street Upper
Dublin 1, D01 C9W8, Ireland

This paperback edition 2022
18

First published in Great Britain by
Collins, The Crime Club 1943

A catalogue record for this book is available from the British Library

ISBN 978-0-00-819654-7 (PB)
ISBN 978-0-00-825577-0 (POD PB)

Set in Sabon LT Std by Palimpsest Book Production Limited,
Falkirk, Stirlingshire
Printed and Bound in the UK using
100% Renewable Electricity at CPI Group (UK) Ltd

To my Friends
Sidney and Mary Smith

CHAPTER 1

When at last I was taken out of the plaster, and the doctors had pulled me about to their hearts' content, and nurses had wheedled me into cautiously using my limbs, and I had been nauseated by their practically using baby talk to me, Marcus Kent told me I was to go and live in the country.

'Good air, quiet life, nothing to do—that's the prescription for you. That sister of yours will look after you. Eat, sleep and imitate the vegetable kingdom as far as possible.'

I didn't ask him if I'd ever be able to fly again. There are questions that you don't ask because you're afraid of the answers to them. In the same way during the last five months I'd never asked if I was going to be condemned to lie on my back all my life. I was afraid of a bright hypocritical reassurance from Sister. 'Come now, *what* a question to ask! We don't let our patients go talking in *that* way!'

So I hadn't asked—and it had been all right. I could move my legs, stand on them, finally walk a few steps—and if I did feel rather like an adventurous baby learning to toddle, with wobbly knees and cotton wool soles to my

1

feet—well, that was only weakness and disuse and would pass.

Marcus Kent, who is the right kind of doctor, answered what I hadn't said.

'You're going to recover completely,' he said. 'We weren't sure until last Tuesday when you had that final overhaul, but I can tell you so authoritatively now. But—it's going to be a long business. A long and, if I may so, a wearisome business. When it's a question of healing nerves and muscles, the brain must help the body. Any impatience, any fretting, will throw you back. And whatever you do, don't "will yourself to get well quickly". Anything of that kind and you'll find yourself back in a nursing home. You've got to take life slowly and easily, the *tempo* is marked *Legato*. Not only has your body got to recover, but your nerves have been weakened by the necessity of keeping you under drugs for so long.

'That's why I say, go down to the country, take a house, get interested in local politics, in local scandal, in village gossip. Take an inquisitive and violent interest in your neighbours. If I may make a suggestion, go to a part of the world where you haven't got any friends scattered about.'

I nodded. 'I had already,' I said, 'thought of that.'

I could think of nothing more insufferable than members of one's own gang dropping in full of sympathy and their own affairs.

'But Jerry, you're looking marvellous—isn't he? Absolutely. Darling, I must tell you—What do you think Buster has done now?'

No, none of that for me. Dogs are wise. They crawl

away into a quiet corner and lick their wounds and do not rejoin the world until they are whole once more.

So it came about that Joanna and I, sorting wildly through house-agents' glowing eulogies of properties all over the British Isles, selected Little Furze, Lymstock, as one of the 'possibles' to be viewed, mainly because we had never been to Lymstock, and knew no one in that neighbourhood.

And when Joanna saw Little Furze she decided at once that it was just the house we wanted.

It lay about half a mile out of Lymstock on the road leading up to the moors. It was a prim low white house, with a sloping Victorian veranda painted a faded green. It had a pleasant view over a slope of heather-covered land with the church spire of Lymstock down below to the left.

It had belonged to a family of maiden ladies, the Misses Barton, of whom only one was left, the youngest, Miss Emily.

Miss Emily Barton was a charming little old lady who matched her house in an incredible way. In a soft apologetic voice she explained to Joanna that she had never let her house before, indeed would never have thought of doing so, 'but you see, my dear, things are so different nowadays—*taxation*, of course, and then my stocks and shares, so *safe*, as I always imagined, and indeed the bank manager *himself* recommended some of them, but they seem to be paying *nothing at all* these days—*foreign*, of course! And really it makes it all so *difficult*. One does not (I'm sure you will understand me, my dear, and not take offence, you look so kind) *like* the idea of letting one's house to strangers—but something must be done, and really, having

seen you, I shall be quite *glad* to think of you being here—
it needs, you know, *young life*. And I must confess I did
shrink from the idea of having *Men* here!'

At this point, Joanna had to break the news of me. Miss
Emily rallied well.

'Oh dear, I see. How sad! A flying accident? So brave,
these young men. Still, your brother will be practically an
invalid—'

The thought seemed to soothe the gentle little lady.
Presumably I should not be indulging in those grosser
masculine activities which Emily Barton feared. She inquired
diffidently if I smoked.

'Like a chimney,' said Joanna. 'But then,' she pointed
out, 'so do I.'

'Of course, of course. So stupid of me. I'm afraid, you
know, I haven't moved with the times. My sisters were all
older than myself, and my dear mother lived to be ninety-
seven—just fancy!—and was most particular. Yes, yes,
everyone smokes now. The only thing is, there are no
ash-trays in the house.'

Joanna said that we would bring lots of ash-trays, and
she added with a smile, 'We won't put down cigarette ends
on your nice furniture, that I do promise you. Nothing
makes me so mad myself as to see people do that.'

So it was settled and we took Little Furze for a period
of six months, with an option of another three, and Emily
Barton explained to Joanna that she herself was going to
be very comfortable because she was going into rooms
kept by an old parlourmaid, 'my faithful Florence', who
had married 'after being with us for fifteen years. *Such* a

nice girl, and her husband is in the building trade. They have a nice house in the High Street and two beautiful rooms on the top floor where I shall be *most* comfortable, and Florence so pleased to have me.'

So everything seemed to be most satisfactory, and the agreement was signed and in due course Joanna and I arrived and settled in, and Miss Emily Barton's maid Partridge having consented to remain, we were well looked after with the assistance of a 'girl' who came in every morning and who seemed to be half-witted but amiable.

Partridge, a gaunt dour female of middle age, cooked admirably, and though disapproving of late dinner (it having been Miss Emily's custom to dine lightly off a boiled egg) nevertheless accommodated herself to our ways and went so far as to admit that she could see I needed my strength building up.

When we had settled in and been at Little Furze a week Miss Emily Barton came solemnly and left cards. Her example was followed by Mrs Symmington, the lawyer's wife, Miss Griffith, the doctor's sister, Mrs Dane Calthrop, the vicar's wife, and Mr Pye of Prior's End.

Joanna was very much impressed.

'I didn't know,' she said in an awestruck voice, 'that people really *called*—with *cards*.'

'That is because, my child,' I said, 'you know nothing about the country.'

'Nonsense. I've stayed away for heaps of week-ends with people.'

'That is not at all the same thing,' I said.

I am five years older than Joanna. I can remember as a

child the big white shabby untidy house we had with the fields running down to the river. I can remember creeping under the nets of raspberry canes unseen by the gardener, and the smell of white dust in the stable yard and an orange cat crossing it, and the sound of horse hoofs kicking something in the stables.

But when I was seven and Joanna two, we went to live in London with an aunt, and thereafter our Christmas and Easter holidays were spent there with pantomimes and theatres and cinemas and excursions to Kensington Gardens with boats, and later to skating rinks. In August we were taken to an hotel by the seaside somewhere.

Reflecting on this, I said thoughtfully to Joanna, and with a feeling of compunction as I realized what a selfish, self-centred invalid I had become:

'This is going to be pretty frightful for you, I'm afraid. You'll miss everything so.'

For Joanna is very pretty and very gay, and she likes dancing and cocktails, and love affairs and rushing about in high-powered cars.

Joanna laughed and said she didn't mind at all.

'As a matter of fact, I'm glad to get away from it all. I really was fed up with the whole crowd, and although you won't be sympathetic, I was really very cut up about Paul. It will take me a long time to get over it.'

I was sceptical over this. Joanna's love affairs always run the same course. She has a mad infatuation for some completely spineless young man who is a misunderstood genius. She listens to his endless complaints and works like anything to get him recognition. Then, when he is ungrateful, she is deeply wounded and says her heart is broken—until the next gloomy young man comes along, which is usually about three weeks later!

So I did not take Joanna's broken heart very seriously. But I did see that living in the country was like a new game to my attractive sister.

'At any rate,' she said, 'I look all right, don't I?'

I studied her critically and was not able to agree.

Joanna was dressed (by Mirotin) for *le Sport*. That is to say she was wearing a skirt of outrageous and preposterous checks. It was skin-tight, and on her upper half she had a ridiculous little short-sleeved jersey with a Tyrolean effect. She had sheer silk stockings and some irreproachable but brand new brogues.

'No,' I said, 'you're all wrong. You ought to be wearing a very old tweed skirt, preferably of dirty green or faded brown. You'd wear a nice cashmere jumper matching it, and perhaps a cardigan coat, and you'd have a felt hat and thick stockings and old shoes. Then, and only then, you'd sink into the background of Lymstock High Street, and not stand out as you do at present.' I added: 'Your face is all wrong, too.'

'What's wrong with that? I've got on my Country Tan Make-up No. 2.'

'Exactly,' I said. 'If you lived in Lymstock, you would have on just a little powder to take the shine off your nose, and possibly a *soupçon* of lipstick—not very well applied— and you would almost certainly be wearing all your eyebrows instead of only a quarter of them.'

Joanna gurgled and seemed much amused.

'Do you think they'll think I'm awful?' she said.

'No,' I said. 'Just queer.'

Joanna had resumed her study of the cards left by our callers. Only the vicar's wife had been so fortunate, or possibly unfortunate, as to catch Joanna at home.

Joanna murmured:

'It's rather like Happy Families, isn't it? Mrs Legal the lawyer's wife, Miss Dose the doctor's daughter, etc.' She added with enthusiasm: 'I do think this is a nice place, Jerry! So sweet and funny and old-world. You just can't think of anything nasty happening here, can you?'

And although I knew what she said was really nonsense, I agreed with her. In a place like Lymstock nothing nasty could happen. It is odd to think that it was just a week later that we got the first letter.

I see that I have begun badly. I have given no description of Lymstock and without understanding what Lymstock is like, it is impossible to understand my story.

To begin with, Lymstock has its roots in the past. Somewhere about the time of the Norman Conquest, Lymstock was a place of importance. That importance was chiefly ecclesiastical. Lymstock had a priory, and it had a long succession of ambitious and powerful priors. Lords and barons in the surrounding countryside made themselves right with Heaven by leaving certain of their lands to the priory. Lymstock Priory waxed rich and important and was a power in the land for many centuries. In due course, however, Henry the Eighth caused it to share the fate of its contemporaries. From then on a castle dominated the town. It was still important. It had rights and privileges and wealth.

And then, somewhere in seventeen hundred and something, the tide of progress swept Lymstock into a backwater. The castle crumbled. Neither railways nor main roads came near Lymstock. It turned into a little provincial market town, unimportant and forgotten, with a sweep of moorland rising behind it, and placid farms and fields ringing it round.

A market was held there once a week, on which day one was apt to encounter cattle in the lanes and roads. It had a small race meeting twice a year which only the most obscure horses attended. It had a charming High Street with dignified houses set flat back, looking slightly incongruous with their ground-floor windows displaying buns or vegetables or fruit. It had a long straggling draper's shop, a large and portentous iron-monger's, a pretentious post office, and a row of straggly indeterminate shops, two rival butchers and an International Stores. It had a doctor, a firm of solicitors, Messrs Galbraith, Galbraith and Symmington, a beautiful and unexpectedly large church dating from fourteen hundred and twenty, with some Saxon remains incorporated in it, a new and hideous school, and two pubs.

Such was Lymstock, and urged on by Emily Barton, anybody who was anybody came to call upon us, and in due course Joanna, having bought a pair of gloves and assumed a velvet beret rather the worse for wear, sallied forth to return them.

To us, it was all quite novel and entertaining. We were not there for life. It was, for us, an interlude. I prepared to obey my doctor's instructions and get interested in my neighbours.

Joanna and I found it all great fun.

I remembered, I suppose, Marcus Kent's instructions to enjoy the local scandals. I certainly didn't suspect how these scandals were going to be introduced to my notice.

The odd part of it was that the letter, when it came, amused us more than anything else.

It arrived, I remember, at breakfast. I turned it over, in the idle way one does when time goes slowly and every event must be spun out to its full extent. It was, I saw, a local letter with a typewritten address.

I opened it before the two with London postmarks, since one of them was a bill and the other from a rather tiresome cousin.

Inside, printed words and letters had been cut out and gummed to a sheet of paper. For a minute or two I stared at the words without taking them in. Then I gasped.

Joanna, who was frowning over some bills, looked up.

'Hallo,' she said, 'what is it? You look quite startled.'

The letter, using terms of the coarsest character, expressed the writer's opinion that Joanna and I were not brother and sister.

'It's a particularly foul anonymous letter,' I said.

I was still suffering from shock. Somehow one didn't expect that kind of thing in the placid backwater of Lymstock.

Joanna at once displayed lively interest.

'*No?* What does it say?'

In novels, I have noticed, anonymous letters of a foul

and disgusting character are never shown, if possible, to women. It is implied that women must at all cost be shielded from the shock it might give their delicate nervous systems.

I am sorry to say it never occurred to me not to show the letter to Joanna. I handed it to her at once.

She vindicated my belief in her toughness by displaying no emotion but that of amusement.

'What an awful bit of dirt! I've always heard about anonymous letters, but I've never seen one before. Are they always like this?'

'I can't tell you,' I said. 'It's my first experience, too.'

Joanna began to giggle.

'You must have been right about my make-up, Jerry. I suppose they think I just *must* be an abandoned female!'

'That,' I said, 'coupled with the fact that our father was a tall, dark lantern-jawed man and our mother a fair-haired blue-eyed little creature, and that I take after him and you take after her.'

Joanna nodded thoughtfully.

'Yes, we're not a bit alike. Nobody would take us for brother and sister.'

'Somebody certainly hasn't,' I said with feeling.

Joanna said she thought it was frightfully funny.

She dangled the letter thoughtfully by one corner and asked what we were to do with it.

'The correct procedure, I believe,' I said, 'is to drop it into the fire with a sharp exclamation of disgust.'

I suited the action to the word, and Joanna applauded.

'You did that beautifully,' she added. 'You ought to have been on the stage. It's lucky we still have fires, isn't it?'

'The waste-paper basket would have been much less dramatic,' I agreed. 'I could, of course, have set light to it with a match and slowly watched it burn—or watched it slowly burn.'

'Things never burn when you want them to,' said Joanna. 'They go out. You'd probably have had to strike match after match.'

She got up and went towards the window. Then, standing there, she turned her head sharply.

'I wonder,' she said, 'who wrote it?'

'We're never likely to know,' I said.

'No—I suppose not.' She was silent a moment, and then said: 'I don't know when I come to think of it that it is so funny after all. You know, I thought they—they *liked* us down here.'

'So they do,' I said. 'This is just some half-crazy brain on the borderline.'

'I suppose so. Ugh—Nasty!'

As she went out into the sunshine I thought to myself as I smoked my after-breakfast cigarette that she was quite right. It was nasty. Someone resented our coming here—someone resented Joanna's bright young sophisticated beauty—somebody wanted to *hurt*. To take it with a laugh was perhaps the best way—but deep down it wasn't funny . . .

Dr Griffith came that morning. I had fixed up for him to give me a weekly overhaul. I liked Owen Griffith. He was dark, ungainly, with awkward ways of moving and deft, very gentle hands. He had a jerky way of talking and was rather shy.

He reported progress to be encouraging. Then he added:

'You're feeling all right, aren't you. Is it my fancy, or are you a bit under the weather this morning?'

'Not really,' I said. 'A particularly scurrilous anonymous letter arrived with the morning coffee, and it's left rather a nasty taste in the mouth.'

He dropped his bag on the floor. His thin dark face was excited.

'Do you mean to say that *you've* had one of them?'

I was interested.

'They've been going about, then?'

'Yes. For some time.'

'Oh,' I said, 'I see. I was under the impression that our presence as strangers was resented here.'

'No, no, it's nothing to do with that. It's just—' He paused and then asked, 'What did it say? At least—' he turned suddenly red and embarrassed—'perhaps I oughtn't to ask?'

'I'll tell you with pleasure,' I said. 'It just said that the fancy tart I'd brought down with me wasn't my sister—not 'alf! And that, I may say, is a Bowdlerized version.'

His dark face flushed angrily.

'How damnable! Your sister didn't—she's not upset, I hope?'

'Joanna,' I said, 'looks a little like the angel off the top of the Christmas tree, but she's eminently modern and quite tough. She found it highly entertaining. Such things haven't come her way before.'

'I should hope not, indeed,' said Griffith warmly.

'And anyway,' I said firmly. 'That's the best way to take it, I think. As something utterly ridiculous.'

'Yes,' said Owen Griffith. 'Only—'

He stopped, and I chimed in quickly: 'Quite so,' I said. 'Only is the word!'

'The trouble is,' he said, 'that this sort of thing, once it starts, grows.'

'So I should imagine.'

'It's pathological, of course.'

I nodded. 'Any idea who's behind it?' I asked.

'No, I wish I had. You see, the anonymous letter pest arises from one of two causes. Either it's *particular*—directed at one particular person or set of people, that is to say it's *motivated*, it's someone who's got a definite grudge (or thinks they have) and who chooses a particularly nasty and underhand way of working it off. It's mean and disgusting but it's not necessarily crazy, and it's usually fairly easy to trace the writer—a discharged servant, a jealous woman—and so on. But if it's *general*, and not particular, then it's more serious. The letters are sent indiscriminately and serve the purpose of working off some frustration in the writer's mind. As I say, it's definitely pathological. And the craze grows. In the end, of course, you track down the person in question—it's often someone extremely unlikely, and that's that. There was a bad outburst of the kind over the other side of the county last year—turned out to be the head of the millinery department in a big draper's establishment. Quiet, refined woman—had been there for years. I remember something of the same kind in my last practice up north—but that turned out to be purely personal spite. Still, as I say, I've seen something of this kind of thing, and, quite frankly, it frightens me!'

'Has it been going on long?' I asked.

'I don't think so. Hard to say, of course, because people who get these letters don't go round advertising the fact. They put them in the fire.'

He paused.

'I've had one myself. Symmington, the solicitor, he's had one. And one or two of my poorer patients have told me about them.'

'All much the same sort of thing?'

'Oh yes. A definite harping on the sex theme. That's always a feature.' He grinned. 'Symmington was accused of illicit relations with his lady clerk—poor old Miss Ginch, who's forty at least, with pince-nez and teeth like a rabbit. Symmington took it straight to the police. My letters accused me of violating professional decorum with my lady patients, stressing the details. They're all quite childish and absurd, but horribly venomous.' His face changed, grew grave. 'But all the same, I'm *afraid*. These things can be dangerous, you know.'

'I suppose they can.'

'You see,' he said, 'crude, childish spite though it is, sooner or later one of these letters will hit the mark. And then, God knows what may happen! I'm afraid, too, of the effect upon the slow, suspicious uneducated mind. If they see a thing written, they believe it's true. All sorts of complications may arise.'

'It was an illiterate sort of letter,' I said thoughtfully, 'written by somebody practically illiterate, I should say.'

'Was it?' said Owen, and went away.

Thinking it over afterwards, I found that 'Was it?' rather disturbing.

CHAPTER 2

I am not going to pretend that the arrival of our anonymous letter did not leave a nasty taste in the mouth. It did. At the same time, it soon passed out of my mind. I did not, you see, at that point, take it seriously. I think I remember saying to myself that these things probably happen fairly often in out-of-the-way villages. Some hysterical woman with a taste for dramatizing herself was probably at the bottom of it. Anyway, if the letters were as childish and silly as the one we had got, they couldn't do much harm.

The next *incident*, if I may put it so, occurred about a week later, when Partridge, her lips set tightly together, informed me that Beatrice, the daily help, would not be coming today.

'I gather, sir,' said Partridge, 'that the girl has been Upset.'

I was not very sure what Partridge was implying, but I diagnosed (wrongly) some stomachic trouble to which Partridge was too delicate to allude more directly. I said I was sorry and hoped she would soon be better.

'The girl is perfectly well, sir,' said Partridge. 'She is Upset in her Feelings.'

'Oh,' I said rather doubtfully.

'Owing,' went on Partridge, 'to a letter she has received. Making, I understand, Insinuations.'

The grimness of Partridge's eye, coupled with the obvious capital I of Insinuations, made me apprehensive that the insinuations were concerned with me. Since I would hardly have recognized Beatrice by sight if I had met her in the town so unaware of her had I been—I felt a not unnatural annoyance. An invalid hobbling about on two sticks is hardly cast for the role of deceiver of village girls. I said irritably:

'What nonsense!'

'My very words, sir, to the girl's mother,' said Partridge. '"Goings On in this house," I said to her, "there never have been and never will be while I am in charge. As to Beatrice," I said, "girls are different nowadays, and as to Goings On elsewhere I can say nothing." But the truth is, sir, that Beatrice's friend from the garage as she walks out with got one of them nasty letters too, and he isn't acting reasonable at all.'

'I have never heard anything so preposterous in my life,' I said angrily.

'It's my opinion, sir,' said Partridge, 'that we're well rid of the girl. What I say is, she wouldn't take on so if there wasn't *something* she didn't want found out. No smoke without fire, that's what I say.'

I had no idea how horribly tired I was going to get of that particular phrase.

*

That morning, by way of adventure, I was to walk down to the village. (Joanna and I always called it the village, although technically we were incorrect, and Lymstock would have been annoyed to hear us.)

The sun was shining, the air was cool and crisp with the sweetness of spring in it. I assembled my sticks and started off, firmly refusing to permit Joanna to accompany me.

'No,' I said, 'I will not have a guardian angel teetering along beside me and uttering encouraging chirrups. A man travels fastest who travels alone, remember. I have much business to transact. I shall go to Galbraith, Galbraith and Symmington, and sign that transfer of shares, I shall call in at the baker's and complain about the currant loaf, and I shall return that book we borrowed. I have to go to the bank, too. Let me away, woman, the morning is all too short.'

It was arranged that Joanna should pick me up with the car and drive me back up the hill in time for lunch.

'That ought to give you time to pass the time of day with everyone in Lymstock.'

'I have no doubt,' I said, 'that I shall have seen anybody who is anybody by then.'

For morning in the High Street was a kind of rendezvous for shoppers, when news was exchanged.

I did not, after all, walk down to the town unaccompanied. I had gone about two hundred yards, when I heard a bicycle bell behind me, then a scrunching of brakes, and then Megan Hunter more or less fell off her machine at my feet.

'Hallo,' she said breathlessly as she rose and dusted herself off.

I rather liked Megan and always felt oddly sorry for her.

She was Symmington the lawyer's step-daughter, Mrs Symmington's daughter by a first marriage. Nobody talked much about Mr (or Captain) Hunter, and I gathered that he was considered best forgotten. He was reported to have treated Mrs Symmington very badly. She had divorced him a year or two after the marriage. She was a woman with means of her own and had settled down with her little daughter in Lymstock 'to forget', and had eventually married the only eligible bachelor in the place, Richard Symmington. There were two boys of the second marriage to whom their parents were devoted, and I fancied that Megan sometimes felt odd man out in the establishment. She certainly did not resemble her mother, who was a small anaemic woman, fadedly pretty, who talked in a thin melancholy voice of servant difficulties and her health.

Megan was a tall awkward girl, and although she was actually twenty, she looked more like a schoolgirlish sixteen. She had a shock of untidy brown hair, hazel green eyes, a thin bony face, and an unexpected charming one-sided smile. Her clothes were drab and unattractive and she usually had on lisle thread stockings with holes in them.

She looked, I decided this morning, much more like a horse than a human being. In fact she would have been a very nice horse with a little grooming.

She spoke, as usual, in a kind of breathless rush.

'I've been up to the farm—you know, Lasher's—to see if they'd got any duck's eggs. They've got an awfully nice lot of little pigs. Sweet! Do you like pigs? I do. I even like the smell.'

'Well-kept pigs shouldn't smell,' I said.

'Shouldn't they? They all do round here. Are you walking down to the town? I saw you were alone, so I thought I'd stop and walk with you, only I stopped rather suddenly.'

'You've torn your stocking,' I said.

Megan looked rather ruefully at her right leg.

'So I have. But it's got two holes already, so it doesn't matter very much, does it?'

'Don't you ever mend your stockings, Megan?'

'Rather. When Mummy catches me. But she doesn't notice awfully what I do—so it's lucky in a way, isn't it?'

'You don't seem to realize you're grown up,' I said.

'You mean I ought to be more like your sister? All dolled up?'

I rather resented this description of Joanna.

'She looks clean and tidy and pleasing to the eye,' I said.

'She's awfully pretty,' said Megan. 'She isn't a bit like you, is she? Why not?'

'Brothers and sisters aren't always alike.'

'No. Of course. I'm not very like Brian or Colin. And Brian and Colin aren't like each other.' She paused and said, 'It's very rum, isn't it?'

'What is?'

Megan replied briefly: 'Families.'

I said thoughtfully, 'I suppose they are.'

I wondered just what was passing in her mind. We walked on in silence for a moment or two, then Megan said in a rather shy voice:

'You fly, don't you?'

'Yes.'

'That's how you got hurt?'

'Yes, I crashed.'

Megan said:

'Nobody down here flies.'

'No,' I said. 'I suppose not. Would you like to fly, Megan?'

'Me?' Megan seemed surprised. 'Goodness, no. I should be sick. I'm sick in a train even.'

She paused, and then asked with that directness which only a child usually displays:

'Will you get all right and be able to fly again, or will you always be a bit of a crock?'

'My doctor says I shall be quite all right.'

'Yes, but is he the kind of man who tells lies?'

'I don't think so,' I replied. 'In fact, I'm quite sure of it. I trust him.'

'That's all right then. But a lot of people do tell lies.'

I accepted this undeniable statement of fact in silence.

Megan said in a detached judicial kind of way:

'I'm glad. I was afraid you looked bad tempered because you were crocked up for life—but if it's just natural, it's different.'

'I'm not bad tempered,' I said coldly.

'Well, irritable, then.'

'I'm irritable because I'm in a hurry to get fit again—and these things can't be hurried.'

'Then why fuss?'

I began to laugh.

21

'My dear girl, aren't you ever in a hurry for things to happen?'

Megan considered the question. She said:

'No. Why should I be? There's nothing to be in a hurry about. Nothing ever happens.'

I was struck by something forlorn in the words. I said gently: 'What do you do with yourself down here?'

She shrugged her shoulders.

'What is there to do?'

'Haven't you got any hobbies? Do you play games? Have you got friends round about?'

'I'm stupid at games. And I don't like them much. There aren't many girls round here, and the ones there are I don't like. They think I'm awful.'

'Nonsense. Why should they?'

Megan shook her head.

'Didn't you go to school at all?'

'Yes, I came back a year ago.'

'Did you enjoy school?'

'It wasn't bad. They taught you things in an awfully silly way, though.'

'How do you mean?'

'Well—just bits and pieces. Chopping and changing from one thing to the other. It was a cheap school, you know, and the teachers weren't very good. They could never answer questions properly.'

'Very few teachers can,' I said.

'Why not? They ought to.'

I agreed.

'Of course I'm pretty stupid,' said Megan. 'And such a

lot of things seem to me such rot. History, for instance. Why, it's quite different out of different books!'

'That is its real interest,' I said.

'And grammar,' went on Megan. 'And silly compositions. And all the blathering stuff Shelley wrote, twittering on about skylarks, and Wordsworth going all potty over some silly daffodils. And Shakespeare.'

'What's wrong with Shakespeare?' I inquired with interest.

'Twisting himself up to say things in such a difficult way that you can't get at what he means. Still, I like *some* Shakespeare.'

'He would be gratified to know that, I'm sure,' I said.

Megan suspected no sarcasm. She said, her face lighting up:

'I like Goneril and Regan, for instance.'

'Why these two?'

'Oh, I don't know. They're *satisfactory*, somehow. Why do you think they were like that?'

'Like what?'

'Like they were. I mean *something* must have made them like that?'

For the first time I wondered. I had always accepted Lear's elder daughters as two nasty bits of goods and had let it go at that. But Megan's demand for a first cause interested me.

'I'll think about it,' I said.

'Oh, it doesn't really matter. I just wondered. Anyway, it's only English Literature, isn't it?'

'Quite, quite. Wasn't there any subject you enjoyed?'

'Only Maths.'

'Maths?' I said, rather surprised.

Megan's face had lit up.

'I loved Maths. But it wasn't awfully well taught. I'd like to be taught Maths really well. It's heavenly. I think there's something heavenly about numbers, anyway, don't you?'

'I've never felt it,' I said truthfully.

We were now entering the High Street. Megan said sharply:

'Here's Miss Griffith. Hateful woman.'

'Don't you like her?'

'I loathe her. She's always at me to join her foul Guides. I hate Guides. Why dress yourself up and go about in clumps, and put badges on yourself for something you haven't really learnt to do properly? I think it's all rot.'

On the whole, I rather agreed with Megan. But Miss Griffith had descended on us before I could voice my assent.

The doctor's sister, who rejoiced in the singularly inappropriate name of Aimée, had all the positive assurance that her brother lacked. She was a handsome woman in a masculine weather-beaten way, with a deep hearty voice.

'Hallo, you two,' she bayed at us. 'Gorgeous morning, isn't it? Megan, you're just the person I wanted to see. I want some help addressing envelopes for the Conservative Association.'

Megan muttered something elusive, propped up her bicycle against the kerb and dived in a purposeful way into the International Stores.

'Extraordinary child,' said Miss Griffith, looking after her. 'Bone lazy. Spends her time mooning about. Must be a great trial to poor Mrs Symmington. I know her mother's tried more than once to get her to take up something—shorthand-typing, you know, or cookery, or keeping Angora rabbits. She needs an *interest* in life.'

I thought that was probably true, but felt that in Megan's place I should have withstood firmly any of Aimée Griffith's suggestions for the simple reason that her aggressive personality would have put my back up.

'I don't believe in idleness,' went on Miss Griffith. 'And certainly not for young people. It's not as though Megan was pretty or attractive or anything like that. Sometimes I think the girl's half-witted. A great disappointment to her mother. The father, you know,' she lowered her voice slightly, 'was definitely a wrong 'un. Afraid the child takes after him. Painful for her mother. Oh, well, it takes all sorts to make a world, that's what I say.'

'Fortunately,' I responded.

Aimée Griffith gave a 'jolly' laugh.

'Yes, it wouldn't do if we were all made to one pattern. But I don't like to see anyone not getting all they can out of life. I enjoy life myself and I want everyone to enjoy it too. People say to me you must be bored to death living down there in the country all the year round. Not a bit of it, I say. I'm always busy, always happy! There's always something going on in the country. My time's taken up, what with my Guides, and the Institute and various committees—to say nothing of looking after Owen.'

At this minute, Miss Griffith saw an acquaintance on

the other side of the street, and uttering a bay of recognition she leaped across the road, leaving me free to pursue my course to the bank.

I always found Miss Griffith rather overwhelming, though I admired her energy and vitality, and it was pleasant to see the beaming contentment with her lot in life which she always displayed, and which was a pleasant contrast to the subdued complaining murmurs of so many women.

My business at the bank transacted satisfactorily, I went on to the offices of Messrs Galbraith, Galbraith and Symmington. I don't know if there were any Galbraiths extant. I never saw any. I was shown into Richard Symmington's inner office which had the agreeable mustiness of a long-established legal firm.

Vast numbers of deed boxes, labelled Lady Hope, Sir Everard Carr, William Yatesby-Hoares, Esq., Deceased, etc., gave the required atmosphere of decorous county families and legitimate long-established business.

Studying Mr Symmington as he bent over the documents I had brought, it occurred to me that if Mrs Symmington had encountered disaster in her first marriage, she had certainly played safe in her second. Richard Symmington was the acme of calm respectability, the sort of man who would never give his wife a moment's anxiety. A long neck with a pronounced Adam's apple, a slightly cadaverous face and a long thin nose. A kindly man, no doubt, a good husband and father, but not one to set the pulses madly racing.

Presently Mr Symmington began to speak. He spoke clearly and slowly, delivering himself of much good sense and shrewd acumen. We settled the matter in hand and I rose to go, remarking as I did so:

'I walked down the hill with your step-daughter.'

For a moment Mr Symmington looked as though he did not know who his step-daughter was, then he smiled.

'Oh yes, of course, Megan. She—er—has been back from school some time. We're thinking about finding her something to do—yes, to do. But of course she's very young still. And backward for her age, so they say. Yes, so they tell me.'

I went out. In the outer office was a very old man on a stool writing slowly and laboriously, a small cheeky-looking boy and a middle-aged woman with frizzy hair and pince-nez who was typing with some speed and dash.

If this was Miss Ginch I agreed with Owen Griffith that tender passages between her and her employer were exceedingly unlikely.

I went into the baker's and said my piece about the currant loaf. It was received with the exclamation and incredulity proper to the occasion, and a new currant loaf was thrust upon me in replacement—'fresh from the oven this minute'—as its indecent heat pressed against my chest proclaimed to be no less than truth.

I came out of the shop and looked up and down the street hoping to see Joanna with the car. The walk had tired me a good deal and it was awkward getting along with my sticks and the currant loaf.

But there was no sign of Joanna as yet.

Suddenly my eyes were held in glad and incredulous surprise.

Along the pavement towards me there came floating a goddess. There is really no other word for it.

The perfect features, the crisply curling golden hair, the tall exquisitely shaped body! And she walked like a goddess, without effort, seeming to swim nearer and nearer. A glorious, an incredible, a breath-taking girl!

In my intense excitement something had to go. What went was the currant loaf. It slipped from my clutches. I made a dive after it and lost my stick, which clattered to the pavement, and I slipped and nearly fell myself.

It was the strong arm of the goddess that caught and held me. I began to stammer:

'Th-thanks awfully, I'm f-f-frightfully sorry.'

She had retrieved the currant loaf and handed it to me together with the stick. And then she smiled kindly and said cheerfully:

'Don't mention it. No trouble, I assure you,' and the magic died completely before the flat, competent voice.

A nice healthy-looking well set-up girl, no more.

I fell to reflecting what would have happened if the Gods had given Helen of Troy exactly those flat accents. How strange that a girl could trouble your inmost soul so long as she kept her mouth shut, and that the moment she spoke the glamour could vanish as though it had never been.

I had known the reverse happen, though. I had seen a little sad monkey-faced woman whom no one would turn to look at twice. Then she opened her mouth and suddenly enchantment had lived and bloomed and Cleopatra had cast her spell anew.

Joanna had drawn up at the kerb beside me without my

noticing her arrival. She asked if there was anything the matter.

'Nothing,' I said, pulling myself together. 'I was reflecting on Helen of Troy and others.'

'What a funny place to do it,' said Joanna. 'You looked *most* odd, standing there clasping currant bread to your breast with your mouth wide open.'

'I've had a shock,' I said. 'I have been transplanted to Ilium and back again.

'Do you know who that is?' I added, indicating a retreating back that was swimming gracefully away.

Peering after the girl Joanna said that it was the Symmingtons' nursery governess.

'Is that what struck you all of a heap?' she asked. 'She's good-looking, but a bit of a wet fish.'

'I know,' I said. 'Just a nice kind girl. And I'd been thinking her Aphrodite.'

Joanna opened the door of the car and I got in.

'It's funny, isn't it?' she said. 'Some people have lots of looks and absolutely no S.A. That girl has. It seems such a pity.'

I said that if she was a nursery governess it was probably just as well.

CHAPTER 3

That afternoon we went to tea with Mr Pye.

Mr Pye was an extremely ladylike plump little man, devoted to his *petit point* chairs, his Dresden shepherdesses and his collection of bric-à-brac. He lived at Prior's Lodge in the grounds of which were the ruins of the old Priory.

Prior's Lodge was certainly a very exquisite house and under Mr Pye's loving care it showed to its best advantage. Every piece of furniture was polished and set in the exact place most suited to it. The curtains and cushions were of exquisite tone and colour, and of the most expensive silks.

It was hardly a man's house, and it did strike me that to live there would be rather like taking up one's abode in a period room at a museum. Mr Pye's principal enjoyment in life was taking people round his house. Even those completely insensitive to their surroundings could not escape. Even if you were so hardened as to consider the essentials of living a radio, a cocktail bar, a bath and a bed surrounded by the necessary walls. Mr Pye did not despair of leading you to better things.

His small plump hands quivered with sensibility as he

described his treasures, and his voice rose to a falsetto squeak as he narrated the exciting circumstances under which he had brought his Italian bedstead home from Verona.

Joanna and I being both fond of antiquities and of period furniture, met with approval.

'It is really a pleasure, a great pleasure, to have such an acquisition to our little community. The dear good people down here, you know, so painfully bucolic—not to say *provincial*. They don't know anything. Vandals—absolute vandals! And the inside of their houses—it would make you weep, dear lady, I assure you it would make you weep. Perhaps it has done so?'

Joanna said that she hadn't gone quite as far as that.

'But you see what I mean? They mix things so terribly! I've seen with my own eyes a most delightful little Sheraton piece—delicate, perfect—a collector's piece, absolutely—and next to it a Victorian occasional table, or quite possibly a fumed oak revolving bookcase—yes, even that—*fumed oak*.'

He shuddered—and murmured plaintively:

'Why are people so blind? You agree—I'm sure you agree, that beauty is the only thing worth living for.'

Hypnotized by his earnestness, Joanna said, yes, yes, that was so.

'Then why,' demanded Mr Pye, 'do people surround themselves with ugliness?'

Joanna said it was very odd.

'Odd? It's *criminal*! That's what I call it—criminal! And the excuses they give! They say something is *comfortable*. Or that it is *quaint*. Quaint! Such a horrible word.'

'The house you have taken,' went on Mr Pye, 'Miss Emily Barton's house. Now that is charming, and she has some quite nice pieces. Quite nice. One or two of them are really first class. And she has taste, too—although I'm not quite so sure of that as I was. Sometimes, I am afraid, I think it's really sentiment. She likes to keep things as they were—but not for *le bon motif*—not because of the resultant harmony—but because it is the way her mother had them.'

He transferred his attention to me, and his voice changed. It altered from that of the rapt artist to that of the born gossip.

'You didn't know the family at all? No, quite so—yes, through house agents. But, my dears, you *ought* to have known that family! When I came here the old mother was still alive. An incredible person—quite incredible! A *monster*, if you know what I mean. Positively a monster. The old-fashioned Victorian monster, devouring her young. Yes, that's what it amounted to. She was monumental, you know, must have weighed seventeen stone, and all the five daughters revolved round her. "The girls"! That's how she always spoke of them. The girls! And the eldest was well over sixty then. "Those stupid girls!" she used to call them sometimes. Slaves, that's all they were, fetching and carrying and agreeing with her. Ten o'clock they had to go to bed and they weren't allowed a fire in their bedroom, and as for asking their own friends to the house, that would have been unheard of. She despised them, you know, for not getting married, and yet so arranged their lives that it was practically impossible for them to meet anybody. I believe

Emily, or perhaps it was Agnes, did have some kind of affair with a curate. But his family wasn't good enough and Mamma soon put a stop to *that*!'

'It sounds like a novel,' said Joanna.

'Oh, my dear, it was. And then the dreadful old woman died, but of course it was far too late *then*. They just went on living there and talking in hushed voices about what poor Mamma would have wished. Even repapering her bedroom they felt to be quite sacrilegious. Still they did enjoy themselves in the parish in a quiet way . . . But none of them had much stamina, and they just died off one by one. Influenza took off Edith, and Minnie had an operation and didn't recover and poor Mabel had a stroke—Emily looked after her in the most devoted manner. Really that poor woman has done nothing but nursing for the last ten years. A charming creature, don't you think? Like a piece of Dresden. So sad for her having financial anxieties—but of course all investments have depreciated.'

'We feel rather awful being in her house,' said Joanna.

'No, no, my dear young lady. You mustn't feel that way. Her dear good Florence is devoted to her and she told me herself how happy she was to have got such nice tenants.' Here Mr Pye made a little bow. 'She told me she thought she had been most fortunate.'

'The house,' I said, 'has a very soothing atmosphere.'

Mr Pye darted a quick glance at me.

'Really? You feel that? Now, that's very interesting. I wondered, you know. Yes, I wondered.'

'What do you mean, Mr Pye?' asked Joanna.

My Pye spread out his plump hands.

'Nothing, nothing. One wondered, that is all. I do believe in atmosphere, you know. People's thoughts and feelings. They give their impression to the walls and the furniture.'

I did not speak for a moment or two. I was looking round me and wondering how I would describe the atmosphere of Prior's Lodge. It seemed to me that the curious thing was that it hadn't any atmosphere! That was really very remarkable.

I reflected on this point so long that I heard nothing of the conversation going on between Joanna and her host. I was recalled to myself, however, by hearing Joanna uttering farewell preliminaries. I came out of my dream and added my quota.

We all went out into the hall. As we came towards the front door a letter came through the box and fell on the mat.

'Afternoon post,' murmured Mr Pye as he picked it up. 'Now, my dear young people, you will come again, won't you? Such a pleasure to meet some broader minds, if you understand me. Someone with an appreciation of Art. Really you know, these dear good people down here, if you mention the Ballet, it conveys to them pirouetting toes, and *tulle* skirts and old gentlemen with opera glasses in the Naughty Nineties. It does indeed. Fifty years behind the times—that's what I put them down, as. A wonderful country, England. It has *pockets*. Lymstock is one of them. Interesting from a collector's point of view—I always feel I have voluntarily put myself under a glass shade when I am here. The peaceful backwater where nothing ever happens.'

Shaking hands with us twice over, he helped me with

exaggerated care into the car. Joanna took the wheel, she negotiated with some care the circular sweep round a plot of unblemished grass, then with a straight drive ahead, she raised a hand to wave goodbye to our host where he stood on the steps of the house. I leaned forward to do the same.

But our gesture of farewell went unheeded. Mr Pye had opened his mail.

He was standing staring down at the open sheet in his hand.

Joanna had described him once as a plump pink cherub. He was still plump, but he was not looking like a cherub now. His face was a dark congested purple, contorted with rage and surprise.

And at that moment I realized that there had been something familiar about the look of that envelope. I had not realized it at the time—indeed it had been one of those things that you note unconsciously without knowing that you do note them.

'Goodness,' said Joanna. 'What's bitten the poor pet?'

'I rather fancy,' I said, 'that it's the Hidden Hand again.'

She turned an astonished face towards me and the car swerved.

'Careful, wench,' I said.

Joanna refixed her attention on the road. She was frowning.

'You mean a letter like the one you got?'

'That's my guess.'

'What is this place?' asked Joanna. 'It looks the most innocent sleepy harmless little bit of England you can imagine—'

'Where to quote Mr Pye, nothing ever happens,' I cut

in. 'He chose the wrong minute to say that. Something has happened.'

'But who writes these things, Jerry?'

I shrugged my shoulders.

'My dear girl, how should I know? Some local nitwit with a screw loose, I suppose.'

'But why? It seems so idiotic.'

'You must read Freud and Jung and that lot to find out. Or ask our Dr Owen.'

Joanna tossed her head.

'Dr Owen doesn't like me.'

'He's hardly seen you.'

'He's seen quite enough, apparently, to make him cross over if he sees me coming along the High Street.'

'A most unusual reaction,' I said sympathetically. 'And one you're not used to.'

Joanna was frowning again.

'No, but seriously, Jerry, why *do* people write anonymous letters?'

'As I say, they've got a screw loose. It satisfies some urge, I suppose. If you've been snubbed, or ignored, or frustrated, and your life's pretty drab and empty, I suppose you get a sense of power from stabbing in the dark at people who are happy and enjoying themselves.'

Joanna shivered. 'Not nice.'

'No, not nice. I should imagine the people in these country places tend to be inbred.'

'Somebody, I suppose, quite uneducated and inarticulate? With better education—'

Joanna did not finish her sentence, and I said nothing.

I have never been able to accept the easy belief that education is a panacea for every ill.

As we drove through the town before climbing up the hill road, I looked curiously at the few figures abroad in the High Street. Was one of those sturdy country-women going about with a load of spite and malice behind her placid brow, planning perhaps even now a further outpouring of vindictive spleen?

But I still did not take the thing seriously.

Two days later we went to a bridge party at the Symmingtons.

It was a Saturday afternoon—the Symmingtons always had their bridge parties on a Saturday, because the office was shut then.

There were two tables. The players were the Symmingtons, ourselves, Miss Griffith, Mr Pye, Miss Barton and a Colonel Appleton whom we had not yet met and who lived at Combeacre, a village some seven miles distant. He was a perfect specimen of the Blimp type, about sixty years of age, liked playing what he called a 'plucky game' (which usually resulted in immense sums above the line being scored by his opponents) and was so intrigued by Joanna that he practically never took his eyes off her the whole afternoon.

I was forced to admit that my sister was probably the most attractive thing that had been seen in Lymstock for many a long day.

When we arrived, Elsie Holland, the children's governess, was hunting for some extra bridge scorers in an ornate writing desk. She glided across the floor with them in the same celestial way I had first noticed, but the spell could not be cast a second time. Exasperating that it should be so—a waste of a perfectly lovely form and face. But I noticed now only too clearly the exceptionally large white teeth like tombstones, and the way she showed her gums when she laughed. She was, unfortunately, one of your prattling girls.

'Are these the ones, Mrs Symmington? It's ever so stupid of me not to remember where we put them away last time. It's my fault, too, I'm afraid. I had them in my hand and then Brian called out his engine had got caught, and I ran out and what with one thing and another I must have just stuffed them in somewhere stupid. These aren't the right ones, I see now, they're a bit yellow at the edges. Shall I tell Agnes tea at five? I'm taking the kiddies to Long Barrow so there won't be any noise.'

A nice kind bright girl. I caught Joanna's eye. She was laughing. I stared at her coldly. Joanna always knows what is passing in my mind, curse her.

We settled down to bridge.

I was soon to know to a nicety the bridge status of everyone in Lymstock. Mrs Symmington was an exceedingly good bridge player and was quite a devotee of the game. Like many definitely unintellectual women, she was not stupid and had a considerable natural shrewdness. Her husband was a good sound player, slightly over-cautious. Mr Pye can best be described as brilliant. He had an uncanny flair for psychic bidding. Joanna and I, since the party was in our honour, played at a table with Mrs Symmington and

Mr Pye. It was Symmington's task to pour oil on troubled waters and by the exercise of tact to reconcile the three other players at his table. Colonel Appleton, as I have said, was wont to play 'a plucky game'. Little Miss Barton was without exception the worst bridge player I have ever come across and always enjoyed herself enormously. She did manage to follow suit, but had the wildest ideas as to the strength of her hand, never knew the score, repeatedly led out of the wrong hand and was quite unable to count trumps and often forgot what they were. Aimée Griffith's play can be summed up in her own words. 'I like a good game of bridge with no nonsense—and I don't play any of these rubbishy conventions. I say what I mean. And no postmortems! After all, it's only a game!' It will be seen, therefore, that their host had not too easy a task.

Play proceeded fairly harmoniously, however, with occasional forgetfulness on the part of Colonel Appleton as he stared across at Joanna.

Tea was laid in the dining-room, round a big table. As we were finishing, two hot and excited little boys rushed in and were introduced, Mrs Symmington beaming with maternal pride, as was their father.

Then, just as we were finishing, a shadow darkened my plate, and I turned my head to see Megan standing in the French window.

'Oh,' said her mother. 'Here's Megan.'

Her voice held a faintly surprised note, as though she had forgotten that Megan existed.

The girl came in and shook hands, awkwardly and without any grace.

'I'm afraid I forgot about your tea, dear,' said Mrs Symmington. 'Miss Holland and the boys took theirs out with them, so there's no nursery tea today. I forgot you weren't with them.'

Megan nodded.

'That's all right. I'll go to the kitchen.'

She slouched out of the room. She was untidily dressed as usual and there were potatoes in both heels.

Mrs Symmington said with a little apologetic laugh:

'My poor Megan. She's just at that awkward age, you know. Girls are always shy and awkward when they've just left school before they're properly grown up.'

I saw Joanna's fair head jerk backwards in what I knew to be a warlike gesture.

'But Megan's twenty, isn't she?' she said.

'Oh, yes, yes. She is. But of course she's very young for her age. Quite a child still. It's so nice, I think, when girls don't grow up too quickly.' She laughed again. 'I expect all mothers want their children to remain babies.'

'I can't think why,' said Joanna. 'After all, it would be a bit awkward if one had a child who remained mentally six while his body grew up.'

'Oh, you mustn't take things so literally, Miss Burton,' said Mrs Symmington.

It occurred to me at that moment that I did not much care for Mrs Symmington. That anaemic, slighted, faded prettiness concealed, I thought, a selfish and grasping nature. She said, and I disliked her a little more still:

'My poor Megan. She's rather a difficult child, I'm afraid. I've been trying to find something for her to do—I believe there are several things one can learn by correspondence. Designing and dressmaking—or she might try and learn shorthand and typing.'

The red glint was still in Joanna's eye. She said as we sat down again at the bridge table:

'I suppose she'll be going to parties and all that sort of thing. Are you going to give a dance for her?'

'A dance?' Mrs Symmington seemed surprised and amused. 'Oh, no, we don't do things like that down here.'

'I see. Just tennis parties and things like that.'

'Our tennis court has not been played on for years. Neither Richard nor I play. I suppose, later, when the boys grow up—Oh, Megan will find plenty to do. She's quite happy just pottering about, you know. Let me see, did I deal? Two No Trumps.'

As we drove home, Joanna said with a vicious pressure on the accelerator pedal that made the car leap forward:

'I feel awfully sorry for that girl.'

'Megan?'

'Yes. Her mother doesn't like her.'

'Oh, come now, Joanna, it's not as bad as that.'

'Yes, it is. Lots of mothers don't like their children. Megan, I should imagine, is an awkward sort of creature to have about the house. She disturbs the pattern—the Symmington pattern. It's a complete unit without her—and that's a most unhappy feeling for a sensitive creature to have—and she *is* sensitive.'

'Yes,' I said, 'I think she is.'

I was silent a moment.

Joanna suddenly laughed mischievously.

'Bad luck for you about the governess.'

'I don't know what you mean,' I said with dignity.

'Nonsense. Masculine chagrin was written on your face every time you looked at her. I agree with you. It is a waste.'

'I don't know what you're talking about.'

'But I'm delighted, all the same. It's the first sign of reviving life. I was quite worried about you at the nursing home. You never even looked at that remarkably pretty nurse you had. An attractive minx, too—absolutely God's gift to a sick man.'

'Your conversation, Joanna, I find definitely low.'

My sister continued without paying the least attention to my remarks.

'So I was much relieved to see you'd still got an eye for a nice bit of skirt. She *is* a good looker. Funny that the S.A. should have been left out completely. It is odd, you know, Jerry. What *is* the thing that some women have and others haven't? What is it makes one woman, even if she only says "Foul weather" so attractive that every man within range wants to come over and talk about the weather with her? I suppose Providence makes a mistake every now and then when sending out the parcel. One Aphrodite face and form, one temperament ditto. And something goes astray and the Aphrodite temperament goes to some little plain-faced creature, and then all the other women go simply mad and say, "I can't think what the men see in her. She isn't even good looking!"'

'Have you quite finished, Joanna?'

'Well, you do agree, don't you?'

I grinned. 'I'll admit to disappointment.'

'And I don't see who else there is here for you. You'll have to fall back upon Aimée Griffith.'

'God forbid,' I said.

'She's quite good looking, you know.'

'Too much of an Amazon for me.'

'She seems to enjoy her life, all right,' said Joanna. 'Absolutely disgustingly hearty, isn't she? I shouldn't be at all surprised if she had a cold bath every morning.'

'And what are you going to do for yourself?' I asked.

'Me?'

'Yes. You'll need a little distraction down here if I know you.'

'Who's being low now? Besides, you forget Paul.' Joanna heaved up a not very convincing sigh.

'I shan't forget him nearly as quickly as you will. In about ten days you'll be saying, "Paul? Paul Who? I never knew a Paul."'

'You think I'm completely fickle,' said Joanna.

'When people like Paul are in question, I'm only too glad that you should be.'

'You never did like him. But he really was a bit of a genius.'

'Possibly, though I doubt it. Anyway, from all I've heard, geniuses are people to be heartily disliked. One thing, you won't find any geniuses down here.'

Joanna considered for a moment, her head on one side. 'I'm afraid not,' she said regretfully.

'You'll have to fall back upon Owen Griffith,' I said. 'He's the only unattached male in the place. Unless you count old Colonel Appleton. He was looking at you like a hungry bloodhound most of the afternoon.'

Joanna laughed.

'He was, wasn't he? It was quite embarrassing.'

'Don't pretend. You're never embarrassed.'

Joanna drove in silence through the gate and round to the garage.

She said then:

'There may be something in that idea of yours.'

'What idea?'

Joanna replied:

'I don't see why any man should deliberately cross the street to avoid me. It's rude, apart from anything else.'

'I see,' I said. 'You're going to hunt the man down in cold blood.'

'Well, I don't like being avoided.'

I got slowly and carefully out of the car, and balanced my sticks. Then I offered my sister a piece of advice.

'Let me tell you this, my girl. Owen Griffith isn't any of your tame whining artistic young men. Unless you're careful you'll stir up a hornet's nest about your ears. That man could be dangerous.'

'Oo, do you think so?' demanded Joanna with every symptom of pleasure at the prospect.

'Leave the poor devil alone,' I said sternly.

'How dare he cross the street when he saw me coming?'

'All you women are alike. You harp on one theme. You'll have Sister Aimée gunning you, too, if I'm not mistaken.'

'She dislikes me already,' said Joanna. She spoke meditatively, but with a certain satisfaction.

'We have come down here,' I said sternly, 'for peace and quiet, and I mean to see we get it.'

But peace and quiet were the last things we were to have.

CHAPTER 4

It was, I think, about a week later, that Partridge informed
me that Mrs Baker would like to speak to me for a minute
or two if I would be so kind.

The name Mrs Baker conveyed nothing at all to me.

'Who is Mrs Baker?' I said, bewildered—'Can't she see
Miss Joanna?'

But it appeared that I was the person with whom an
interview was desired. It further transpired that Mrs Baker
was the mother of the girl Beatrice.

I had forgotten Beatrice. For a fortnight now, I had been
conscious of a middle-aged woman with wisps of grey hair,
usually on her knees retreating crablike from bathroom
and stairs and passages when I appeared, and I knew, I
suppose, that she was our new Daily Woman. Otherwise
the Beatrice complication had faded from my mind.

I could not very well refuse to see Beatrice's mother,
especially as I learned that Joanna was out, but I was, I
must confess, a little nervous at the prospect. I sincerely
hoped that I was not going to be accused of having trifled
with Beatrice's affections. I cursed the mischievous activities

of anonymous letter writers to myself at the same time as, aloud, I commanded that Beatrice's mother should be brought to my presence.

Mrs Baker was a big broad weather-beaten woman with a rapid flow of speech. I was relieved to notice no signs of anger or accusation.

'I hope, sir,' she said, beginning at once when the door had closed behind Partridge, 'that you'll excuse the liberty I've taken in coming to see you. But I thought, sir, as you was the proper person to come to, and I should be thankful if you could see your way to telling me what I ought to do in the circumstances, because in my opinion, sir, something ought to be done, and I've never been one to let the grass grow under my feet, and what I say is, no use moaning and groaning, but "Up and doing" as vicar said in his sermon only the week before last.'

I felt slightly bewildered and as though I had missed something essential in the conversation.

'Certainly,' I said. 'Won't you—er—sit down, Mrs Baker? I'm sure I shall be glad to—er help you in any way I can—'

I paused expectantly.

'Thank you, sir.' Mrs Baker sat down on the edge of a chair. 'It's very good of you, I'm sure. And glad I am that I came to you, I said to Beatrice, I said, and her howling and crying on her bed, Mr Burton will know what to do, I said, being a London gentleman. And something must be done, what with young men being so hot-headed and not listening to reason the way they are, and not listening to a word a girl says, and anyway, if it was *me*, I says to

Beatrice I'd give him as good as I got, and what about that girl down at the mill?'

I felt more than ever bewildered.

'I'm sorry,' I said. 'But I don't quite understand. What has happened?'

'It's the letters, sir. Wicked letters—indecent, too, using such words and all. Worse than I've ever seen in the Bible, even.'

Passing over an interesting side-line here, I said desperately:

'Has your daughter been having more letters?'

'Not her, sir. She had just the one. That one as was the occasion of her leaving here.'

'There was absolutely no reason—' I began, but Mrs Baker firmly and respectfully interrupted me:

'There is no need to tell me, sir, that what was wrote was all wicked lies. I had Miss Partridge's word for that—and indeed I would have known it for myself. You aren't that type of gentleman, sir, that I well know, and you an invalid and all. Wicked untruthful lies it was, but all the same I says to Beatrice as she'd better leave because you know what talk is, sir. No smoke without fire, that's what people say. And a girl can't be too careful. And besides the girl herself felt bashful like after what had been written, so I says, "Quite right," to Beatrice when she said she wasn't coming up here again, though I'm sure we both regretted the inconvenience being such—'

Unable to find her way out of this sentence, Mrs Baker took a deep breath and began again.

'And that, I hoped, would be the end of any nasty talk. But now George, down at the garage, him what Beatrice is going with, he's got one of them. Saying awful things about our Beatrice, and how she's going on with Fred Ledbetter's Tom—and I can assure you, sir, the girl has been no more than civil to him and passing the time of day so to speak.'

My head was now reeling under this new complication of Mr Ledbetter's Tom.

'Let me get this straight,' I said. 'Beatrice's—er—young man has had an anonymous letter making accusations about her and another young man?'

'That's right, sir, and not nicely put at all—horrible words used, and it drove young George mad with rage, it did, and he came round and told Beatrice he wasn't going to put up with that sort of thing from her, and he wasn't going to have her go behind his back with other chaps—and she says it's all a lie—and he says no smoke without fire, he says, and rushes off being hot-like in his temper, and Beatrice she took on ever so, poor girl, and I said I'll put my hat on and come straight up to you, sir.'

Mrs Baker paused and looked at me expectantly, like a dog waiting for reward after doing a particularly clever trick.

'But why come to me?' I demanded.

'I understood, sir, that you'd had one of these nasty letters yourself, and I thought, sir, that being a London gentleman, you'd know what to do about them.'

'If I were you,' I said, 'I should go to the police. This sort of thing ought to be stopped.'

Mrs Baker looked deeply shocked.

'Oh, no, sir. I couldn't go to the police.'

'Why not?'

'I've never been mixed up with the police, sir. None of us ever have.'

'Probably not. But the police are the only people who can deal with this sort of thing. It's their business.'

'Go to Bert Rundle?'

Bert Rundle was the constable, I knew.

'There's a sergeant, or an inspector, surely, at the police station.'

'Me, go into the police station?'

Mrs Baker's voice expressed reproach and incredulity. I began to feel annoyed.

'That's the only advice I can give you.'

Mrs Baker was silent, obviously quite unconvinced. She said wistfully and earnestly:

'These letters ought to be stopped, sir, they did ought to be stopped. There'll be mischief done sooner or later.'

'It seems to me there is mischief done now,' I said.

'I meant *violence*, sir. These young fellows, they get violent in their feelings—and so do the older ones.'

I asked:

'Are a good many of these letters going about?'

Mrs Baker nodded.

'It's getting worse and worse, sir. Mr and Mrs Beadle at the Blue Boar—very happy they've always been—and now these letters comes and it sets him thinking things— things that aren't so, sir.'

I leaned forward:

'Mrs Baker,' I said, 'have you any idea, any idea at all, who is writing these abominable letters?'

To my great surprise she nodded her head.

'We've got our idea, sir. Yes, we've all got a very fair idea.'

'Who is it?'

I had fancied she might be reluctant to mention a name, but she replied promptly:

''Tis Mrs Cleat—that's what we all think, sir. 'Tis Mrs Cleat for sure.'

I had heard so many names this morning that I was quite bewildered. I asked:

'Who is Mrs Cleat?'

Mrs Cleat, I discovered, was the wife of an elderly jobbing gardener. She lived in a cottage on the road leading down to the Mill. My further questions only brought unsatisfactory answers. Questioned as to why Mrs Cleat should write these letters, Mrs Baker would only say vaguely that ''Twould be like her.'

In the end I let her go, reiterating once more my advice to go to the police, advice which I could see Mrs Baker was not going to act upon. I was left with the impression that I had disappointed her.

I thought over what she had said. Vague as the evidence was, I decided that if the village was all agreed that Mrs Cleat was the culprit, then it was probably true. I decided to go and consult Griffith about the whole thing. Presumably he would know this Cleat woman. If he thought advisable, he or I might suggest to the police that she was at the bottom of this growing annoyance.

I timed my arrival for about the moment I fancied Griffith

would have finished his 'Surgery'. When the last patient had left, I went into the surgery.

'Hallo, it's you, Burton.'

'Yes. I want to talk to you.'

I outlined my conversation with Mrs Baker, and passed on to him the conviction that this Mrs Cleat was responsible. Rather to my disappointment, Griffith shook his head.

'It's not so simple as that,' he said.

'You don't think this Cleat woman is at the bottom of it?'

'She may be. But I should think it most unlikely.'

'Then why do they all think it is her?'

He smiled.

'Oh,' he said, 'you don't understand. Mrs Cleat is the local witch.'

'Good gracious!' I exclaimed.

'Yes, sounds rather strange nowadays, nevertheless that's what it amounts to. The feeling lingers, you know, that there are certain people, certain families, for instance, whom it isn't wise to offend. Mrs Cleat came from a family of "wise women". And I'm afraid she's taken pains to cultivate the legend. She's a queer woman with a bitter and sardonic sense of humour. It's been easy enough for her, if a child cut its finger, or had a bad fall, or sickened with mumps, to nod her head and say, "Yes, he stole my apples last week" or "He pulled my cat's tail." Soon enough mothers pulled their children away, and other women brought honey or a cake they'd baked to give to Mrs Cleat so as to keep on the right side of her so that she shouldn't "ill wish" them. It's superstitious and silly, but it happens. So naturally, now, they think she's at the bottom of this.'

'But she isn't?'

'Oh, no. She isn't the type. It's—it's not so simple as that.'

'Have you any idea?' I looked at him curiously.

He shook his head, but his eyes were absent.

'No,' he said. 'I don't know at all. But I don't like it, Burton—some harm is going to come of this.'

When I got back to the house I found Megan sitting on the veranda steps, her chin resting on her knees.

She greeted me with her usual lack of ceremony.

'Hallo,' she said. 'Do you think I could come to lunch?'

'Certainly,' I said.

'If it's chops, or anything difficult like that and they won't go round, just tell me,' shouted Megan as I went round to apprize Partridge of the fact that there would be three to lunch.

I fancy that Partridge sniffed. She certainly managed to convey without saying a word of any kind, that she didn't think much of that Miss Megan.

I went back to the veranda.

'Is it quite all right?' asked Megan anxiously.

'Quite all right,' I said. 'Irish stew.'

'Oh well, that's rather like dogs' dinner anyway, isn't it? I mean it's mostly potato and flavour.'

'Quite,' I said.

I took out my cigarette case and offered it to Megan. She flushed.

'How nice of you.'

'Won't you have one?'

'No, I don't think I will, but it was very nice of you to offer it to me—just as though I was a real person.'

'Aren't you a real person?' I said amused.

Megan shook her head, then, changing the subject, she stretched out a long dusty leg for my inspection.

'I've darned my stockings,' she announced proudly.

I am not an authority on darning, but it did occur to me that the strange puckered blot of violently contrasting wool was perhaps not quite a success.

'It's much more uncomfortable than the hole,' said Megan.

'It looks as though it might be,' I agreed.

'Does your sister darn well?'

I tried to think if I had ever observed any of Joanna's handiwork in this direction.

'I don't know,' I had to confess.

'Well, what does she do when she gets a hole in her stocking?'

'I rather think,' I said reluctantly, 'that she throws them away and buys another pair.'

'Very sensible,' said Megan. 'But I can't do that. I get an allowance now—forty pounds a year. You can't do much on that.'

I agreed.

'If only I wore black stockings, I could ink my legs,' said Megan sadly. 'That's what I always did at school. Miss Batworthy, the mistress who looked after our mending was like her name—blind as a bat. It was awfully useful.'

'It must have been,' I said.

We were silent while I smoked my pipe. It was quite a companionable silence.

Megan broke it by saying suddenly and violently:

'I suppose you think I'm awful, like everyone else?'

I was so startled that my pipe fell out of my mouth. It was a meerschaum, just colouring nicely, and it broke. I said angrily to Megan:

'Now, see what you've done.'

That most unaccountable of children, instead of being upset, merely grinned broadly.

'I do like you,' she said.

It was a most warming remark. It is the remark that one fancies perhaps erroneously that one's dog would say if he could talk. It occurred to me that Megan, for all she looked like a horse, had the disposition of a dog. She was certainly not quite human.

'What did you say before the catastrophe?' I asked, carefully picking up the fragments of my cherished pipe.

'I said I supposed you thought me awful,' said Megan, but not at all in the same tone she had said it before.

'Why should I?'

Megan said gravely:

'Because I am.'

I said sharply:

'Don't be stupid.'

Megan shook her head.

'That's just it. I'm not really stupid. People think I am. They don't know that inside I know just what they're like, and that all the time I'm hating them.'

'*Hating* them?'

'Yes,' said Megan.

Her eyes, those melancholy, unchildlike eyes, stared straight into mine, without blinking. It was a long mournful gaze.

'You would hate people if you were like me,' she said. 'If you weren't wanted.'

'Don't you think you're being rather morbid?' I asked.

'Yes,' said Megan. 'That's what people always say when you're saying the truth. And it is true. I'm not wanted and I can quite see why. Mummie doesn't like me a bit. I remind her, I think, of my father, who was cruel to her and pretty dreadful from all I can hear. Only mothers can't say they don't want their children and just go away. Or eat them. Cats eat the kittens they don't like. Awfully sensible, I think. No waste or mess. But human mothers have to keep their children, and look after them. It hasn't been so bad while I could be sent away to school—but you see, what Mummie would really like is to be just herself and my stepfather and the boys.'

I said slowly:

'I still think you're morbid, Megan, but accepting some of what you say as true, why don't you go away and have a life of your own?'

She gave me an unchildlike smile.

'You mean take up a career. Earn my living?'

'Yes.'

'What at?'

'You could train for something, I suppose. Shorthand typing—book-keeping.'

'I don't believe I could. I am stupid about doing things. And besides—'

'Well?'

She had turned her face away, now she turned it slowly back again. It was crimson and there were tears in her eyes. She spoke now with all the childishness back in her voice.

'Why should I go away? And be made to go away? They don't want me, but I'll *stay*. I'll stay and make everyone sorry. I'll make them all sorry. Hateful pigs! I hate everyone here in Lymstock. They all think I'm stupid and ugly. I'll show them. I'll show them. I'll—'

It was a childish, oddly pathetic rage.

I heard a step on the gravel round the corner of the house.

'Get up,' I said savagely. 'Go into the house through the drawing-room. Go up to the first floor to the bathroom. End of the passage. Wash your face. Quick.'

She sprang awkwardly to her feet and darted through the window as Joanna came round the corner of the house.

'Gosh, I'm hot,' she called out. She sat down beside me and fanned her face with the Tyrolean scarf that had been round her head. 'Still I think I'm educating these damned brogues now. I've walked miles. I've learnt one thing, you shouldn't have these fancy holes in your brogues. The gorse prickles go through. Do you know, Jerry, I think we ought to have a dog?'

'So do I,' I said. 'By the way, Megan is coming to lunch.'

'Is she? Good.'

'You like her?' I asked.

'I think she's a changeling,' said Joanna. 'Something left on a doorstep, you know, while the fairies take the right one away. It's very interesting to meet a changeling. Oof, I must go up and wash.'

'You can't yet,' I said, 'Megan is washing.'

'Oh, she's been foot-slogging too, has she?'

Joanna took out her mirror and looked at her face long and earnestly. 'I don't think I like this lipstick,' she announced presently.

Megan came out through the window. She was composed, moderately clean, and showed no signs of the recent storm. She looked doubtfully at Joanna.

'Hallo,' said Joanna, still preoccupied by her face. 'I'm so glad you've come to lunch. Good gracious, I've got a freckle on my nose. I must do something about it. Freckles are so earnest and Scottish.'

Partridge came out and said coldly that luncheon was served.

'Come on,' said Joanna, getting up. 'I'm starving.'

She put her arm through Megan's and they went into the house together.

CHAPTER 5

I see that there has been one omission in my story. So far I have made little or no mention of Mrs Dane Calthrop, or indeed of the Rev. Caleb Dane Calthrop.

And yet both the vicar and his wife were distinct personalities. Dane Calthrop himself was perhaps a being more remote from everyday life than anyone I have ever met. His existence was in his books and in his study, and in his intimate knowledge of early Church history. Mrs Dane Calthrop, on the other hand, was quite terrifyingly on the spot. I have perhaps purposely put off mentioning her, because I was from the first a little afraid of her. She was a woman of character and of almost Olympian knowledge. She was not in the least the typical vicar's wife—but that, as I set it down, makes me ask myself, what do I know of vicars' wives?

The only one I remember well was a quiet nondescript creature, devoted to a big strong husband with a magnetic way of preaching. She had so little general conversation that it was a puzzle to know how to sustain a conversation with her.

Otherwise I was depending on the fictional presentment

of vicars' wives, caricatures of females poking their noses everywhere, and uttering platitudes. Probably no such type exists.

Mrs Dane Calthrop never poked her nose in anywhere, yet she had an uncanny power of knowing things and I soon discovered that almost everyone in the village was slightly afraid of her. She gave no advice and never interfered, yet she represented, to any uneasy conscience, the Deity personified.

I have never seen a woman more indifferent to her material surroundings. On hot days she would stride about clad in Harris tweed, and in rain or even sleet, I have seen her absent-mindedly race down the village street in a cotton dress of printed poppies. She had a long thin well-bred face like a greyhound, and a most devastating sincerity of speech.

She stopped me in the High Street the day after Megan had come to lunch. I had the usual feeling of surprise, because Mrs Dane Calthrop's progress resembled coursing more than walking, and her eyes were always fixed on the distant horizon so that you felt sure her real objective was about a mile and a half away.

'Oh,' she said. 'Mr Burton!'

She said it rather triumphantly, as someone might who had solved a particularly clever puzzle.

I admitted that I was Mr Burton and Mrs Dane Calthrop stopped focusing on the horizon and seemed to be trying to focus on me instead.

'Now what,' she said, 'did I want to see you about?'

I could not help her there. She stood frowning, deeply perplexed.

'Something rather nasty,' she said.

'I'm sorry about that,' I said, startled.

'Ah,' cried Mrs Dane Calthrop. 'I hate my love with an A. That's it. Anonymous letters! What's this story you've brought down here about anonymous letters?'

'I didn't bring it,' I said. 'It was here already.'

'Nobody got any until you came, though,' said Mrs Dane Calthrop accusingly.

'But they did, Mrs Dane Calthrop. The trouble had already started.'

'Oh dear,' said Mrs Dane Calthrop. 'I don't like that.'

She stood there, her eyes absent and far away again. She said:

'I can't help feeling it's all *wrong*. We're not like that here. Envy, of course, and malice, and all the mean spiteful little sins—but I didn't think there was anyone who would do that—No, I really didn't. And it distresses me, you see, because *I* ought to know.'

Her fine eyes came back from the horizon and met mine. They were worried, and seemed to hold the honest bewilderment of a child.

'How should you know?' I said.

'I usually do. I've always felt that's my function. Caleb preaches good sound doctrine and administers the sacraments. That's a priest's duty, but if you admit marriage at all for a priest, then I think his wife's duty is to know what people are feeling and thinking, even if she can't do anything about it. And I haven't the least idea whose mind is—'

She broke off, adding absently.

'They are such silly letters, too.'

'Have you—er—had any yourself?'

I was a little diffident of asking, but Mrs Dane Calthrop replied perfectly naturally, her eyes opening a little wider:

'Oh yes, two—no, three. I forget exactly what they said. Something very silly about Caleb and the school-mistress, I think. Quite absurd, because Caleb has absolutely no taste for fornication. He never has had. So lucky, being a clergyman.'

'Quite,' I said. 'Oh quite.'

'Caleb would have been a saint,' said Mrs Dane Calthrop, 'if he hadn't been just a little too intellectual.'

I did not feel qualified to answer this criticism, and anyway Mrs Dane Calthrop went on, leaping back from her husband to the letters in rather a puzzling way.

'There are so many things the letters might say, but don't. That's what is so curious.'

'I should hardly have thought they erred on the side of restraint,' I said bitterly.

'But they don't seem to *know* anything. None of the real things.'

'You mean?'

Those fine vague eyes met mine.

'Well, of course. There's plenty of adultery here—and everything else. Any amount of shameful secrets. Why doesn't the writer use those?' She paused and then asked abruptly, 'What did they say in your letter?'

'They suggested that my sister wasn't my sister.'

'And she is?'

Mrs Dane Calthrop asked the question with unembarrassed friendly interest.

'Certainly Joanna is my sister.'

Mrs Dane Calthrop nodded her head.

'That just shows you what I mean. I dare say there are other things—'

Her clear uninterested eyes looked at me thoughtfully, and I suddenly understood why Lymstock was afraid of Mrs Dane Calthrop.

In everybody's life there are hidden chapters which they hope may never be known. I felt that Mrs Dane Calthrop knew them.

For once in my life, I was positively delighted when Aimée Griffith's hearty voice boomed out:

'Hallo, Maud. Glad I've just caught you. I want to suggest an alteration of date for the Sale of Work. Morning, Mr Burton.'

She went on:

'I must just pop into the grocer's and leave my order, then I'll come along to the Institute if that suits you?'

'Yes, yes, that will do quite well,' said Mrs Dane Calthrop.

Aimée Griffith went into the International Stores.

Mrs Dane Calthrop said: 'Poor thing.'

I was puzzled. Surely she could not be pitying Aimée?

She went on, however:

'You know, Mr Burton, I'm rather afraid—'

'About this letter business?'

'Yes, you see it means—it must mean—' She paused lost in thought, her eyes screwed up. Then she said slowly, as one who solves a problem, 'Blind hatred . . . yes, blind hatred. But even a blind man might stab to the heart by

63

pure chance . . . And what would happen then, Mr Burton?'

We were to know that before another day had passed.

It was Partridge who brought the news of the tragedy. Partridge enjoys calamity. Her nose always twitches ecstatically when she has to break bad news of any kind.

She came into Joanna's room with her nose working overtime, her eyes bright, and her mouth pulled down into an exaggerated gloom. 'There's terrible news, this morning, miss,' she observed as she drew up the blinds.

It takes a minute or two for Joanna, with her London habits, to become fully conscious in the morning. She said, 'Er ah,' and rolled over without real interest.

Partridge placed her early tea beside her and began again.

'Terrible it is. Shocking! I couldn't hardly believe it when I heard.'

'What's terrible?' said Joanna, struggling into wakefulness.

'Poor Mrs Symmington.' She paused dramatically. 'Dead.'

'Dead?' Joanna sat up in bed, now wide awake.

'Yes, miss, yesterday afternoon, and what's worse, took her own life.'

'Oh no, Partridge?'

Joanna was really shocked—Mrs Symmington was not, somehow, the sort of person you associated with tragedies.

'Yes, miss, it's the truth. Did it deliberate. Not but what she was drove to it, poor soul.'

'Drove to it?' Joanna had an inkling of the truth then. 'Not—?'

Her eyes questioned Partridge and Partridge nodded.

'That's right, miss. One of them nasty letters!'

'What did it say?'

But that, to Partridge's regret, she had not succeeded in learning.

'They're beastly things,' said Joanna. 'But I don't see why they should make one want to kill oneself.'

Partridge sniffed and then said with meaning:

'Not unless they were *true*, miss.'

'Oh,' said Joanna.

She drank her tea after Partridge had left the room, then she threw on a dressing-gown and came in to me to tell me the news.

I thought of what Owen Griffith had said. Sooner or later the shot in the dark went home. It had done with Mrs Symmington. She, apparently the most unlikely of women, had had a secret . . . It was true, I reflected, that for all her shrewdness she was not a woman of much stamina. She was the anaemic clinging type that crumples easily.

Joanna nudged me and asked me what I was thinking about.

I repeated to her what Owen had said.

'Of course,' said Joanna waspishly, 'he would know all about it. That man thinks he knows everything.'

'He's clever,' I said.

'He's conceited,' said Joanna. She added, 'Abominably conceited!'

After a minute or two she said:

'How awful for her husband—and for the girl. What do you think Megan will feel about it?'

I hadn't the slightest idea and said so. It was curious that one could never gauge what Megan would think or feel.

Joanna nodded and said:

'No, one never does know with changelings.'

After a minute or two she said:

'Do you think—would you like—I wonder if she'd like to come and stay with us for a day or two? It's rather a shock for a girl that age.'

'We might go along and suggest it,' I agreed.

'The children are all right,' said Joanna. 'They've got that governess woman. But I expect she's just the sort of creature that would drive someone like Megan mad.'

I thought that was very possible. I could imagine Elsie Holland uttering platitude after platitude and suggesting innumerable cups of tea. A kindly creature, but not, I thought, the person for a sensitive girl.

I had thought myself of bringing Megan away, and I was glad that Joanna had thought of it spontaneously without prompting from me.

We went down to the Symmingtons' house after breakfast.

We were a little nervous, both of us. Our arrival might look like sheer ghoulish curiosity. Luckily we met Owen Griffith just coming out through the gate. He looked worried and preoccupied.

He greeted me, however, with some warmth.

'Oh, hallo, Burton. I'm glad to see you. What I was afraid would happen sooner or later has happened. A damnable business!'

'Good morning, Dr Griffith,' said Joanna, using the voice she keeps for one of our deafer aunts.

Griffith started and flushed.

'Oh—oh, good morning, Miss Burton.'

'I thought perhaps,' said Joanna, 'that you didn't see me.'

Owen Griffith got redder still. His shyness enveloped him like a mantle.

'I'm—I'm so sorry—preoccupied—I didn't.'

Joanna went on mercilessly: 'After all, I *am* life size.'

'Merely kit-kat,' I said in a stern aside to her. Then I went on:

'My sister and I, Griffith, wondered whether it would be a good thing if the girl came and stopped with us for a day or two? What do you think? I don't want to butt in—but it must be rather grim for the poor child. What would Symmington feel about it, do you think?'

Griffith turned the idea over in his mind for a moment or two.

'I think it would be an excellent thing,' he said at last. 'She's a queer nervy sort of girl, and it would be good for her to get away from the whole thing. Miss Holland is doing wonders—she's an excellent head on her shoulders, but she really has quite enough to do with the two children and Symmington himself. He's quite broken up—bewildered.'

'It was—' I hesitated—'suicide?'

Griffith nodded.

'Oh yes. No question of accident. She wrote, "I can't go on" on a scrap of paper. The letter must have come by yesterday afternoon's post. The envelope was down on the floor by her chair and the letter itself was screwed up into a ball and thrown into the fireplace.'

'What did—'

I stopped, rather horrified at myself.

'I beg your pardon,' I said.

Griffith gave a quick unhappy smile.

'You needn't mind asking. That letter will have to be read at the inquest. No getting out of it, more's the pity. It was the usual kind of thing—couched in the same foul style. The specific accusation was that the second boy, Colin, was not Symmington's child.'

'Do you think that was true?' I exclaimed incredulously.

Griffith shrugged his shoulders.

'I've no means of forming a judgment. I've only been here five years. As far as I've ever seen, the Symmingtons were a placid, happy couple devoted to each other and their children. It's true that the boy doesn't particularly resemble his parents—he's got bright red hair, for one thing—but a child often throws back in appearance to a grandfather or grandmother.'

'That lack of resemblance might have been what prompted the particular accusation. A foul and quite uncalled-for bow at a venture.'

'Very likely. In fact, probably. There's not been much accurate knowledge behind these poison pen letters, just unbridled spite and malice.'

'But it happened to hit the bull's eye,' said Joanna. 'After all, she wouldn't have killed herself otherwise, would she?'

Griffith said doubtfully:

'I'm not quite sure. She's been ailing in health for some time, neurotic, hysterical. I've been treating her for a nervous condition. It's possible, I think, that the shock of receiving such a letter, couched in those terms, may have induced such a state of panic and despondency that she may have decided to take her life. She may have worked herself up to feel that her husband might not believe her if she denied the story, and the general shame and disgust might have worked upon her so powerfully as to temporarily unbalance her judgment.'

'Suicide whilst of unsound mind,' said Joanna.

'Exactly. I shall be quite justified, I think, in putting forward that point of view at the inquest.'

'I see,' said Joanna.

There was something in her voice which made Owen say:

'Perfectly justified!' in an angry voice. He added, 'You don't agree, Miss Burton?'

'Oh yes, I do,' said Joanna. 'I'd do exactly the same in your place.'

Owen looked at her doubtfully, then moved slowly away down the street. Joanna and I went on into the house.

The front door was open and it seemed easier than ringing the bell, especially as we heard Elsie Holland's voice inside.

She was talking to Mr Symmington who, huddled in a chair, was looking completely dazed.

'No, but really, Mr Symmington, you must take something. You haven't had any breakfast, not what I call a proper breakfast, and nothing to eat last night, and what with the shock and all, you'll be getting ill yourself, and you'll need all your strength. The doctor said so before he left.'

Symmington said in a toneless voice:

'You're very kind, Miss Holland, but—'

'A nice cup of hot tea,' said Elsie Holland, thrusting the beverage on him firmly.

Personally I should have given the poor devil a stiff whisky and soda. He looked as though he needed it. However, he accepted the tea, and looking up at Elsie Holland:

'I can't thank you for all you've done and are doing, Miss Holland. You've been perfectly splendid.'

The girl flushed and looked pleased.

'It's nice of you to say that, Mr Symmington. You must let me do all I can to help. Don't worry about the children— I'll see to them, and I've got the servants calmed down, and if there's anything I can do, letter-writing or telephoning, don't hesitate to ask me.'

'You're very kind,' Symmington said again.

Elsie Holland, turning, caught sight of us and came hurrying out into the hall.

'Isn't it terrible?' she said in a hushed whisper.

I thought, as I looked at her, that she was really a very nice girl. Kind, competent, practical in an emergency. Her magnificent blue eyes were just faintly rimmed with pink, showing that she had been soft-hearted enough to shed tears for her employer's death.

'Can we speak to you a minute?' asked Joanna. 'We don't want to disturb Mr Symmington.'

Elsie Holland nodded comprehendingly and led the way into the dining-room on the other side of the hall.

'It's been awful for him,' she said. 'Such a shock. Who ever would have thought a thing like this could happen? But of course, I do realize now that she had been queer for some time. Awfully nervy and weepy. I thought it was her health, though Dr Griffith always said there was nothing really wrong with her. But she was snappy and irritable and some days you wouldn't know just how to take her.'

'What we really came for,' said Joanna, 'was to know whether we could have Megan for a few days—that, is if she'd like to come.'

Elsie Holland looked rather surprised.

'Megan?' she said doubtfully. 'I don't know, I'm sure. I mean, it's ever so kind of you, but she's such a queer girl. One never knows what she's going to say or feel about things.'

Joanna said rather vaguely:

'We thought it might be a help, perhaps.'

'Oh well, as far as that goes, it would. I mean, I've got the boys to look after (they're with Cook just now) and poor Mr Symmington—he really needs looking after as much as anyone, and such a lot to do and see to. I really haven't had time to see much to Megan. I think she's upstairs in the old nursery at the top of the house. She seems to want to get away from everyone. I don't know if—'

Joanna gave me the faintest of looks. I slipped quickly out of the room and upstairs.

The old nursery was at the top of the house. I opened the door and went in. The room downstairs had given on to the garden behind and the blinds had not been down there. But in this room which faced the road they were decorously drawn down.

Through a dim grey gloom I saw Megan. She was crouching on a divan set against the far wall, and I was reminded at once of some terrified animal, hiding. She looked petrified with fear.

'Megan,' I said.

I came forward, and unconsciously I adopted the tone one does adopt when you want to reassure a frightened animal. I'm really surprised I didn't hold out a carrot or a piece of sugar. I felt like that.

She stared at me, but she did not move, and her expression did not alter.

'Megan,' I said again. 'Joanna and I have come to ask you if you would like to come and stay with us for a little.'

Her voice came hollowly out of the dim twilight.

'Stay with you? In your house?'

'Yes.'

'You mean, you'll take me away from here?'

'Yes, my dear.'

Suddenly she began to shake all over. It was frightening and very moving.

'Oh, do take me away! Please do. It's so awful, being here, and feeling so wicked.'

I came over to her and her hands fastened on my coat sleeve.

'I'm an awful coward. I didn't know what a coward I was.'

'It's all right, funny face,' I said. 'These things are a bit shattering. Come along.'

'Can we go at once? Without waiting a minute?'

'Well, you'll have to put a few things together, I suppose.'

'What sort of things? Why?'

'My dear girl,' I said. 'We can provide you with a bed and a bath and the rest of it, but I'm damned if I lend you my toothbrush.'

She gave a very faint weak little laugh.

'I see. I think I'm stupid today. You mustn't mind. I'll go and pack some things. You—you won't go away? You'll wait for me?'

'I'll be on the mat.'

'Thank you. Thank you very much. I'm sorry I'm so stupid. But you see it's rather dreadful when your mother dies.'

'I know,' I said.

I gave her a friendly pat on the back and she flashed me a grateful look and disappeared into a bedroom. I went on downstairs.

'I found Megan,' I said. 'She's coming.'

'Oh now, that *is* a good thing,' exclaimed Elsie Holland. 'It will take her out of herself. She's rather a nervy girl, you know. Difficult. It will be a great relief to feel I haven't got her on my mind as well as everything else. It's very kind of you, Miss Burton. I hope she won't be a nuisance. Oh dear, there's the telephone. I must go and answer it. Mr Symmington isn't fit.'

She hurried out of the room. Joanna said:

'Quite the ministering angel!'

'You said that rather nastily,' I observed. 'She's a nice kind girl, and obviously most capable.'

'Most. And she knows it.'

'This is unworthy of you, Joanna,' I said.

'Meaning why shouldn't the girl do her stuff?'

'Exactly.'

'I never can stand seeing people pleased with themselves,' said Joanna. 'It arouses all my worst instincts. How did you find Megan?'

'Crouching in a darkened room looking rather like a stricken gazelle.'

'Poor kid. She was quite willing to come?'

'She leapt at it.'

A series of thuds out in the hall announced the descent of Megan and her suitcase. I went out and took it from her. Joanna, behind me, said urgently:

'Come on. I've already refused some nice hot tea twice.'

We went out to the car. It annoyed me that Joanna had to sling the suitcase in. I could get along with one stick now, but I couldn't do any athletic feats.

'Get in,' I said to Megan.

She got in, I followed her. Joanna started the car and we drove off.

We got to Little Furze and went into the drawing-room.

Megan dropped into a chair and burst into tears. She cried with the hearty fervour of a child—bawled, I think, is the right word. I left the room in search of a remedy. Joanna stood by feeling rather helpless, I think.

Presently I heard Megan say in a thick choked voice:

'I'm sorry for doing this. It seems idiotic.'

Joanna said kindly, 'Not at all. Have another handkerchief.'

I gather she supplied the necessary article. I re-entered the room and handed Megan a brimming glass.

'What is it?'

'A cocktail,' I said.

'Is it? Is it really?' Megan's tears were instantly dried. 'I've never drunk a cocktail.'

'Everything has to have a beginning,' I said.

Megan sipped her drink gingerly, then a beaming smile spread over her face, she tilted her head back and gulped it down at a draught.

'It's lovely,' she said. 'Can I have another?'

'No,' I said.

'Why not?'

'In about ten minutes you'll probably know.'

'Oh!'

Megan transferred her attention to Joanna.

'I really am awfully sorry for having made such a nuisance of myself howling away like that. I can't think why. It seems awfully silly when I'm so glad to be here.'

'That's all right,' said Joanna. 'We're very pleased to have you.'

'You can't be, really. It's just kindness on your part. But I am grateful.'

'Please don't be grateful,' said Joanna. 'It will embarrass me. I was speaking the truth when I said we should be glad to have you. Jerry and I have used up all our conversation. We can't think of any more things to say to each other.'

'But now,' I said, 'we shall be able to have all sorts of interesting discussions—about Goneril and Regan and things like that.'

Megan's face lit up.

'I've been thinking about that, and I think I know the answer. It was because that awful old father of theirs always insisted on such a lot of sucking up. When you've always got to be saying thank you and how kind and all the rest of it, it would make you go a bit rotten and queer inside, and you'd just long to be able to be beastly for a change—and when

75

you got the chance, you'd probably find it went to your head and you'd go too far. Old Lear was pretty awful, wasn't he? I mean, he did deserve the snub Cordelia gave him.'

'I can see,' I said, 'that we are going to have many interesting discussions about Shakespeare.'

'I can see you two are going to be very highbrow,' said Joanna. 'I'm afraid I always find Shakespeare terribly dreary. All those long scenes where everybody is drunk and it's supposed to be funny.'

'Talking of drink,' I said turning to Megan. 'How are you feeling?'

'Quite all right, thank you.'

'Not at all giddy? You don't see two of Joanna or anything like that?'

'No. I just feel as though I'd like to talk rather a lot.'

'Splendid,' I said. 'Obviously you are one of our natural drinkers. That is to say, if that really was your first cocktail.'

'Oh, it was.'

'A good strong head is an asset to any human being,' I said.

Joanna took Megan upstairs to unpack.

Partridge came in, looking sour, and said she had made two cup custards for lunch and what should she do about it?

CHAPTER 6

The inquest was held three days later. It was all done as decorously as possible, but there was a large attendance and, as Joanna observed, the beady bonnets were wagging.

The time of Mrs Symmington's death was put at between three and four o'clock. She was alone in the house, Symmington was at his office, the maids were having their day out, Elsie Holland and the children were out walking and Megan had gone for a bicycle ride.

The letter must have come by the afternoon post. Mrs Symmington must have taken it out of the box, read it—and then in a state of agitation she had gone to the potting shed, fetched some of the cyanide kept there for taking wasps' nests, dissolved it in water and drunk it after writing those last agitated words, 'I can't go on . . .'

Owen Griffith gave medical evidence and stressed the view he had outlined to us of Mrs Symmington's nervous condition and poor stamina. The coroner was suave and discreet. He spoke with bitter condemnation of people who write those despicable things, anonymous letters. Whoever had written that wicked and lying letter was morally guilty of murder, he said. He hoped the police would soon discover the culprit and take action against him or her. Such a dastardly and malicious piece of spite deserved to be punished with the utmost rigour of the law. Directed by him, the jury brought in the inevitable verdict. Suicide whilst temporarily insane.

The coroner had done his best—Owen Griffith also, but afterwards, jammed in the crowd of eager village women, I heard the same hateful sibilant whisper I had begun to know so well, 'No smoke without fire, that's what *I* say!' 'Must 'a been something in it for certain sure. She wouldn't never have done it otherwise . . .'

Just for a moment I hated Lymstock and its narrow boundaries, and its gossiping whispering women.

It is difficult to remember things in their exact chronological order. The next landmark of importance, of course, was Superintendent Nash's visit. But it was before that, I think, that we received calls from various members of the community, each of which was interesting in its way and shed some light on the characters and personalities of the people involved.

Aimée Griffith came on the morning after the inquest. She was looking, as always, radiant with health and vigour and succeeded, also as usual, in putting my back up almost immediately. Joanna and Megan were out, so I did the honours.

'Good morning,' said Miss Griffith. 'I hear you've got Megan Hunter here?'

'We have.'

'Very good of you, I'm sure. It must be rather a nuisance to you. I came up to say she can come to us if you like. I dare say I can find ways of making her useful about the house.'

I looked at Aimée Griffith with a good deal of distaste.

'How good of you,' I said. 'But we like having her. She potters about quite happily.'

'I dare say. Much too fond of pottering, that child. Still, I suppose she can't help it, being practically half-witted.'

'I think she's rather an intelligent girl,' I said.

Aimée Griffith gave me a hard stare.

'First time I've ever heard any one say that of her,' she remarked. 'Why, when you talk to her, she looks through you as though she doesn't understand what you are saying!'

'She probably just isn't interested,' I said.

'If so, she's extremely rude,' said Aimée Griffith.

'That may be. But not half-witted.'

Miss Griffith declared sharply:

'At best, it's wool-gathering. What Megan needs is good hard work—something to give her an interest in life. You've no idea what a difference that makes to a girl. I know a lot about girls. You'd be surprised at the difference even becoming a Guide makes to a girl. Megan's much too old to spend her time lounging about and doing nothing.'

'It's been rather difficult for her to do anything else so far,' I said. 'Mrs Symmington always seemed under the impression that Megan was about twelve years old.'

Miss Griffith snorted.

'I know. I had no patience with that attitude of hers. Of

79

course she's dead now, poor woman, so one doesn't want to say much, but she was a perfect example of what I call the unintelligent domestic type. Bridge and gossip and her children—and even there that Holland girl did all the looking after them. I'm afraid I never thought very much of Mrs Symmington, although of course I never suspected the truth.'

'The truth?' I said sharply.

Miss Griffith flushed.

'I was terribly sorry for Dick Symmington, its all having to come out as it did at the inquest,' she said. 'It was awful for him.'

'But surely you heard him say that there was not a word of truth in that letter—that he was quite sure of that?'

'Of course he *said* so. Quite right. A man's got to stick up for his wife. Dick would.' She paused and then explained: 'You see, I've known Dick Symmington a long time.'

I was a little surprised.

'Really?' I said. 'I understood from your brother that he only bought this practice a few years ago.'

'Oh yes, but Dick Symmington used to come and stay in our part of the world up north. I've known him for years.'

Women jump to conclusions that men do not. Nevertheless, the suddenly softened tone of Aimée Griffith's voice put, as our old nurse would have expressed it, ideas into my head.

I looked at Aimée curiously. She went on—still in that softened tone:

'I know Dick very well . . . He's a proud man, and very

reserved. But he's the sort of man who could be very jealous.'

'That would explain,' I said deliberately, 'why Mrs Symmington was afraid to show him or tell him about the letter. She was afraid that, being a jealous man, he might not believe her denials.'

Miss Griffith looked at me angrily and scornfully.

'Good Lord,' she said, 'do you think any woman would go and swallow a lot of cyanide of potassium for an accusation that wasn't true?'

'The coroner seemed to think it was possible. Your brother, too—'

Aimée interrupted me.

'Men are all alike. All for preserving the decencies. But you don't catch *me* believing that stuff. If an innocent woman gets some foul anonymous letter, she laughs and chucks it away. That's what I—' she paused suddenly, and then finished, 'would do.'

But I had noticed the pause. I was almost sure that what she had been about to say was 'That's what I did.'

I decided to take the war into the enemy's country.

'I see,' I said pleasantly, 'so you've had one, too?'

Aimée Griffith was the type of woman who scorns to lie. She paused a minute—flushed, then said:

'Well, yes. But I didn't let it worry me!'

'Nasty?' I inquired sympathetically, as a fellow-sufferer.

'Naturally. These things always are. The ravings of a lunatic. I read a few words of it, realized what it was and chucked it straight into the waste-paper basket.'

'You didn't think of taking it to the police?'

'Not then. Least said soonest mended—that's what I felt.'

An urge came over me to say solemnly: 'No smoke without fire!' but I restrained myself. To avoid temptation I reverted to Megan.

'Have you any idea of Megan's financial position?' I asked. 'It's not idle curiosity on my part. I wondered if it would actually be necessary for her to earn her living.'

'I don't think it's strictly *necessary*. Her grandmother, her father's mother, left her a small income, I believe. And in any case Dick Symmington would always give her a home and provide for her, even if her mother hasn't left her anything outright. No, it's the *principle* of the thing.'

'What principle?'

'Work, Mr Burton. There's nothing like work, for men and women. The one unforgivable sin is idleness.'

'Sir Edward Grey,' I said, 'afterwards our foreign minister, was sent down from Oxford for incorrigible idleness. The Duke of Wellington, I have heard, was both dull and inattentive at his books. And has it ever occurred to you, Miss Griffith, that you would probably not be able to take a good express train to London if little Georgie Stephenson had been out with his youth movement instead of lolling about, bored, in his mother's kitchen until the curious behaviour of the kettle lid attracted the attention of his idle mind?'

Aimée merely snorted.

'It is a theory of mine,' I said, warming to my theme, 'that we owe most of our great inventions and most of the achievements of genius to idleness—either enforced or

82

voluntary. The human mind prefers to be spoon-fed with the thoughts of others, but deprived of such nourishment it will, reluctantly, begin to think for itself—and such thinking, remember, is original thinking and may have valuable results.

'Besides,' I went on, before Aimée could get in another sniff, 'there is the artistic side.'

I got up and took from my desk where it always accompanied me a photograph of my favourite Chinese picture. It represents an old man sitting beneath a tree playing cat's cradle with a piece of string on his fingers and toes.

'It was in the Chinese exhibition,' I said. 'It fascinated me. Allow me to introduce you. It is called "Old Man enjoying the Pleasures of Idleness".'

Aimée Griffith was unimpressed by my lovely picture. She said: 'Oh well, we all know what the Chinese are like!'

'It doesn't appeal to you?' I asked.

'Frankly, no. I'm not very interested in art, I'm afraid. Your attitude, Mr Burton, is typical of that of most men. You dislike the idea of women working—of their competing——'

I was taken aback. I had come up against the Feminist. Aimée was well away, her cheeks flushed.

'It is incredible to you that women should want a career. It was incredible to my parents. I was anxious to study for a doctor. They would not hear of paying the fees. But they paid them readily for Owen. Yet I should have made a better doctor than my brother.'

'I'm sorry about that,' I said. 'It was tough on you. If one wants to do a thing—'

She went on quickly:

'Oh, I've got over it now. I've plenty of will-power. My life is busy and active. I'm one of the happiest people in Lymstock. Plenty to do. But I do go up in arms against the silly old-fashioned prejudice that women's place is always the home.'

'I'm sorry if I offended you,' I said. 'And that wasn't really my point. I don't see Megan in a domestic role at all.'

'No, poor child. She'll be a misfit anywhere, I'm afraid.' Aimée had calmed down. She was speaking quite normally again. 'Her father, you know—'

She paused and I said bluntly: 'I *don't* know. Everyone says "her father" and drops their voice, and that is that. What did the man *do*? Is he alive still?'

'I really don't know. And I'm rather vague myself, I'm afraid. But he was definitely a bad lot. Prison, I believe. And a streak of very strong abnormality. That's why it wouldn't surprise me if Megan was a bit "wanting".'

'Megan,' I said, 'is in full possession of her senses, and as I said before, I consider her an intelligent girl. My sister thinks so too. Joanna is very fond of her.'

Aimée said:

'I'm afraid your sister must find it very dull down here.'

And as she said it, I learnt something else. Aimée Griffith disliked my sister. It was there in the smooth conventional tones of her voice.

'We've all wondered how you could both bear to bury yourselves in such an out-of-the-way spot.'

It was a question and I answered it.

'Doctor's orders. I was to come somewhere very quiet where nothing ever happened.' I paused and added, 'Not quite true of Lymstock now.'

'No, no, indeed.'

She sounded worried and got up to go. She said then:

'You know—it's got to be put a stop to—all this beastliness! We can't have it going on.'

'Aren't the police doing anything?'

'I suppose so. But I think we ought to take it in hand *ourselves*.'

'We're not as well equipped as they are.'

'Nonsense! We probably have far more sense and intelligence! A little determination is all that is needed.'

She said goodbye abruptly and went away.

When Joanna and Megan came back from their walk I showed Megan my Chinese picture. Her face lighted up. She said, 'It's heavenly, isn't it?'

'That *is* rather my opinion.'

Her forehead was crinkling in the way I knew so well.

'But it would be difficult, wouldn't it?'

'To be idle?'

'No, not to be idle—but to enjoy the pleasures of it. You'd have to be very old—'

She paused. I said: 'He *is* an old man.'

'I don't mean old that way. Not *age*. I mean old in—in . . .'

85

'You mean,' I said, 'that one would have to attain a very high state of civilization for the thing to present itself to you in that way—a fine point of sophistication? I think I shall complete your education, Megan, by reading to you one hundred poems translated from the Chinese.'

I met Symmington in the town later in the day.

'Is it quite all right for Megan to stay on with us for a bit?' I asked. 'It's company for Joanna—she's rather lonely sometimes with none of her own friends.'

'Oh—er—Megan? Oh yes, very good of you.'

I took a dislike to Symmington then which I never quite overcame. He had so obviously forgotten all about Megan. I wouldn't have minded if he had actively disliked the girl—a man may sometimes be jealous of a first husband's child—but he didn't dislike her, he just hardly noticed her. He felt towards her much as a man who doesn't care much for dogs would feel about a dog in the house. You notice it when you fall over it and swear at it, and you give it a vague pat sometimes when it presents itself to be patted. Symmington's complete indifference to his step-daughter annoyed me very much.

I said, 'What are you planning to do with her?'

'With Megan?' He seemed rather startled. 'Well, she'll go on living at home. I mean, naturally, it is her home.'

My grandmother, of whom I had been very fond, used to sing old-fashioned songs to her guitar. One of them, I remembered, ended thus:

'Oh maid, most dear, I am not here
　　I have no place, no part,
No dwelling more, by sea nor shore,
　　But only in your heart.'

I went home humming it.

Emily Barton came just after tea had been cleared away.

She wanted to talk about the garden. We talked garden for about half an hour. Then we turned back towards the house.

It was then that lowering her voice, she murmured:

'I do hope that that child—that she hasn't been too much *upset* by all this dreadful business?'

'Her mother's death, you mean?'

'That, of course. But I really meant, the—the unpleasantness *behind* it.'

I was curious. I wanted Miss Barton's reaction.

'What do you think about that? Was it true?'

'Oh, no, no, surely not. I'm quite sure that Mrs Symmington never—that he wasn't'—little Emily Barton was pink and confused—'I mean it's quite untrue—although of course it may have been a judgment.'

'A judgment?' I said, staring.

Emily Barton was very pink, very Dresden china shepherdess-like.

'I cannot help feeling that all these dreadful letters, all the sorrow and pain they have caused, may have been sent for a *purpose*.'

'They were sent for a purpose, certainly,' I said grimly.

'No, no, Mr Burton, you misunderstood me. I'm not talking of the misguided creature who wrote them—someone quite abandoned that must be. I mean that they have been permitted—by Providence! To awaken us to a sense of our shortcomings.'

'Surely,' I said, 'the Almighty could choose a less unsavoury weapon.'

Miss Emily murmured that God moved in a mysterious way.

'No,' I said. 'There's too much tendency to attribute to God the evils that man does of his own free will. I might concede you the Devil. God doesn't really need to punish us, Miss Barton. We're so very busy punishing ourselves.'

'What I can't make out is *why* should anyone want to do such a thing?'

I shrugged my shoulders.

'A warped mentality.'

'It seems very sad.'

'It doesn't seem to me sad. It seems to me just damnable. And I don't apologize for the word. I mean just that.'

The pink had gone out of Miss Barton's cheeks. They were very white.

'But why, Mr Burton, *why*? What pleasure can anyone get out of it?'

'Nothing you and I can understand, thank goodness.'

Emily Barton lowered her voice.

'They say that *Mrs Cleat*—but I really cannot believe it.'

I shook my head. She went on in an agitated manner:

'Nothing of this kind has ever happened before—never in my memory. It has been such a happy little community. What would my dear mother have said? Well, one must be thankful that she has been spared.'

I thought from all I had heard that old Mrs Barton had been sufficiently tough to have taken anything, and would probably have enjoyed this sensation.

Emily went on:

'It distresses me deeply.'

'You've not—er—had anything yourself?'

She flushed crimson.

'Oh, no—oh, no, indeed. Oh! that would be dreadful.'

I apologized hastily, but she went away looking rather upset.

I went into the house. Joanna was standing by the drawing-room fire which she had just lit, for the evenings were still chilly.

She had an open letter in her hand.

She turned her head quickly as I entered.

'Jerry! I found this in the letter box—dropped in by hand. It begins, "You painted trollop . . ."'

'What else does it say?'

Joanna gave a wide grimace.

'Same old muck.'

She dropped it on to the fire. With a quick gesture that hurt my back I jerked it off again just before it caught.

'Don't,' I said. 'We may need it.'

'Need it?'

'For the police.'

*

89

Agatha Christie

Superintendent Nash came to see me the following morning. From the first moment I saw him I took a great liking to him. He was the best type of C.I.D. county superintendent. Tall, soldierly, with quiet reflective eyes and a straight-forward unassuming manner.

He said: 'Good morning, Mr Burton, I expect you can guess what I've come to see you about.'

'Yes, I think so. This letter business.'

He nodded.

'I understand you had one of them?'

'Yes, soon after we got here.'

'What did it say exactly?'

I thought a minute, then conscientiously repeated the wording of the letter as closely as possible.

The superintendent listened with an immovable face, showing no signs of any kind of emotion. When I had finished, he said:

'I see. You didn't keep the letter, Mr Burton?'

'I'm sorry. I didn't. You see, I thought it was just an isolated instance of spite against newcomers to the place.'

The superintendent inclined his head comprehendingly.

He said briefly: 'A pity.'

'However,' I said, 'my sister got one yesterday. I just stopped her putting it in the fire.'

'Thank you, Mr Burton, that was thoughtful of you.'

I went across to my desk and unlocked the drawer in which I had put it. It was not, I thought, very suitable for Partridge's eyes. I gave it to Nash.

He read it through. Then he looked up and asked me: 'Is this the same in appearance as the last one?'

90

'I think so—as far as I can remember.'

'The same difference between the envelope and the text?'

'Yes,' I said. 'The envelope was typed. The letter itself had printed words pasted on to a sheet of paper.'

Nash nodded and put it in his pocket. Then he said:

'I wonder, Mr Burton, if you would mind coming down to the station with me? We could have a conference there and it would save a good deal of time and overlapping.'

'Certainly,' I said. 'You would like me to come now?'

'If you don't mind.'

There was a police car at the door. We drove down in it. I said:

'Do you think you'll be able to get to the bottom of this?'

Nash nodded with easy confidence.

'Oh yes, we'll get to the bottom of it all right. It's a question of time and routine. They're slow, these cases, but they're pretty sure. It's a matter of narrowing things down.'

'Elimination?' I said.

'Yes. And general routine.'

'Watching post boxes, examining typewriters, fingerprints, all that?'

He smiled. 'As you say.'

At the police station I found Symmington and Griffith were already there. I was introduced to a tall lantern-jawed man in plain clothes, Inspector Graves.

'Inspector Graves,' explained Nash, 'has come down from London to help us. He's an expert on anonymous letter cases.'

Inspector Graves smiled mournfully. I reflected that a life spent in the pursuit of anonymous letter writers must be singularly depressing. Inspector Graves, however, showed a kind of melancholy enthusiasm.

'They're all the same, these cases,' he said in a deep lugubrious voice like a depressed bloodhound. 'You'd be surprised. The wording of the letters and the things they say.'

'We had a case just on two years ago,' said Nash. 'Inspector Graves helped us then.'

Some of the letters, I saw, were spread out on the table in front of Graves. He had evidently been examining them.

'Difficulty is,' said Nash, 'to get hold of the letters. Either people put them in the fire, or they won't admit to having received anything of the kind. Stupid, you see, and afraid of being mixed up with the police. They're a backward lot here.'

'Still we've got a fair amount to get on with,' said Graves. Nash took the letter I had given him from his pocket and tossed it over to Graves.

The latter glanced through it, laid it with the others and observed approvingly:

'Very nice—very nice indeed.'

It was not the way I should have chosen to describe the epistle in question, but experts, I suppose, have their own point of view. I was glad that that screed of vituperative and obscene abuse gave *somebody* pleasure.

'We've got enough, I think, to go on with,' said Inspector Graves, 'and I'll ask you gentlemen, if you should get any more, to bring them along at once. Also, if you hear of someone else getting one—(you, in particular, doctor, among your patients) do your best to get them to come along here with them. I've got—' he sorted with deft fingers among his exhibits, 'one to Mr Symmington, received as far back as two months ago, one to Dr Griffith, one to Miss Ginch, one written to Mrs Mudge, the butcher's wife, one to Jennifer Clark, barmaid at the Three Crowns, the one received by Mrs Symmington, this one now to Miss Burton—oh yes, and one from the bank manager.'

'Quite a representative collection,' I remarked.

'And not one I couldn't match from other cases! This one here is as near as nothing to one written by that milliner woman. This one is the dead spit of an outbreak we had up in Northumberland—written by a schoolgirl, they were. I can tell you, gentlemen, I'd like to see something *new* sometimes, instead of the same old treadmill.'

'There is nothing new under the sun,' I murmured.

'Quite so, sir. You'd know that if you were in our profession.'

Nash sighed and said, 'Yes, indeed.'

Symmington asked:

'Have you come to any definite opinion as to the writer?'

Graves cleared his throat and delivered a small lecture.

'There are certain similarities shared by all these letters. I shall enumerate them, gentlemen, in case they suggest anything to your minds. The text of the letters is composed of words made up from individual letters cut out of a printed book. It's an old book, printed, I should say, about the year 1830. This has obviously been done to avoid the risk of recognition through handwriting which is, as most people know nowadays, a fairly easy matter . . . the so-called disguising of a hand not amounting to much when faced with expert tests. There are no fingerprints on the letters and envelopes of a distinctive character. That is to say, they have been handled by the postal authorities, the recipient, and there are other stray fingerprints, but no set common to all, showing therefore that the person who put them together was careful to wear gloves. The envelopes are typewritten by a Windsor 7 machine, well worn, with the a and the t out of alignment. Most of them have been posted locally, or put in the box of a house by hand. It is therefore evident that they are of local provenance. They were written by a woman, and in my opinion a woman of middle age or over, and probably, though not certainly, unmarried.'

We maintained a respectful silence for a minute or two. Then I said:

'The typewriter's your best bet, isn't it? That oughtn't to be difficult in a little place like this.'

Inspector Graves shook his head sadly and said:

'That's where you're wrong, sir.'

'The typewriter,' said Superintendent Nash, 'is unfortunately too easy. It is an old one from Mr Symmington's office, given by him to the Women's Institute where, I may say, it's fairly easy of access. The ladies here all often go into the Institute.'

'Can't you tell something definite from the—er—the touch, don't you call it?'

Again Graves nodded.

'Yes, that can be done—but these envelopes have all been typed by someone using one finger.'

'Someone, then, unused to the typewriter?'

'No, I wouldn't say that. Someone, say, who can type but doesn't want us to know the fact.'

'Whoever writes these things has been very cunning,' I said slowly.

'She is, sir, she is,' said Graves. 'Up to every trick of the trade.'

'I shouldn't have thought one of these bucolic women down here would have had the brains,' I said.

Graves coughed.

'I haven't made myself plain, I'm afraid. Those letters were written by an educated woman.'

'What, by a lady?'

The word slipped out involuntarily. I hadn't used the term 'lady' for years. But now it came automatically to my lips, re-echoed from days long ago, and my grandmother's faint unconsciously arrogant voice saying, 'Of course, she isn't a *lady*, dear.'

Nash understood at once. The word lady still meant something to him.

'Not necessarily a lady,' he said. 'But certainly not a village woman. They're mostly pretty illiterate down here, can't spell, and certainly can't express themselves with fluency.'

I was silent, for I had had a shock. The community was so small. Unconsciously I had visualized the writer of the letters as a Mrs Cleat or her like, some spiteful, cunning half-wit.

Symmington put my thoughts into words. He said sharply:

'But that narrows it down to about half a dozen to a dozen people in the whole place!'

'That's right.'

'I can't believe it.'

Then, with a slight effort, and looking straight in front of him as though the mere sound of his own words was distasteful, he said:

'You have heard what I stated at the inquest. In case you may have thought that that statement was actuated by a desire to protect my wife's memory, I should like to repeat now that I am firmly convinced that the subject matter of the letter my wife received was absolutely false. I *know* it was false. My wife was a very sensitive woman, and—er—well, you might call it *prudish* in some respects. Such a letter would have been a great shock to her, and she was in poor health.'

Graves responded instantly.

'That's quite likely to be right, sir. None of these letters show any signs of intimate knowledge. They're just blind accusations. There's been no attempt to blackmail. And there doesn't seem to be any religious bias—such as we sometimes get. It's just sex and spite! And that's going to give us quite a good pointer towards the writer.'

Symmington got up. Dry and unemotional as the man was, his lips were trembling.

'I hope you find the devil who writes these soon. She murdered my wife as surely as if she'd put a knife into her.' He paused. 'How does she feel now, I wonder?'

He went out, leaving that question unanswered.

'How does she feel, Griffith?' I asked. It seemed to me the answer was in his province.

'God knows. Remorseful, perhaps. On the other hand, it may be that she's enjoying her power. Mrs Symmington's death may have fed her mania.'

'I hope not,' I said, with a slight shiver. 'Because if so, she'll—'

I hesitated and Nash finished the sentence for me.

'She'll try it again? That, Mr Burton, would be the best thing that could happen, for us. The pitcher goes to the well once too often, remember.'

'She'd be mad to go on with it,' I exclaimed.

'She'll go on,' said Graves. 'They always do. It's a vice, you know, they can't let it alone.'

I shook my head with a shudder. I asked if they needed me any longer, I wanted to get out into the air. The atmosphere seemed tinged with evil.

'There's nothing more, Mr Burton,' said Nash. 'Only keep your eyes open, and do as much propaganda as you can—that is to say, urge on everyone that they've got to report any letter they receive.'

I nodded.

'I should think everyone in the place has had one of the foul things by now,' I said.

'I wonder,' said Graves. He put his sad head a little on one side and asked, 'You don't know, definitely, of anyone who *hasn't* had a letter?'

'What an extraordinary question! The population at large isn't likely to take me into their confidence.'

'No, no, Mr Burton, I didn't mean that. I just wondered if you knew of any one person who quite definitely, to your certain knowledge, has not received an anonymous letter.'

'Well, as a matter of fact,' I hesitated, 'I do, in a way.'

And I repeated my conversation with Emily Barton and what she had said.

Graves received the information with a wooden face and said: 'Well, that may come in useful. I'll note it down.'

I went out into the afternoon sunshine with Owen Griffith. Once in the street, I swore aloud.

'What kind of place is this for a man to come to lie in the sun and heal his wounds? It's full of festering poison, this place, and it looks as peaceful and as innocent as the Garden of Eden.'

'Even there,' said Owen dryly, 'there was one serpent.'

'Look here, Griffith, do they know anything? Have they got any idea?'

'I don't know. They've got a wonderful technique, the police. They're seemingly so frank, and they tell you nothing.'

'Yes. Nash is a nice fellow.'

'And a very capable one.'

'If anyone's batty in this place, *you* ought to know it.' I said accusingly.

Griffith shook his head. He looked discouraged. But he looked more than that—he looked worried. I wondered if he had an inkling of some kind.

We had been walking along the High Street. I stopped at the door of the house agents.

'I believe my second instalment of rent is due—in advance. I've got a good mind to pay it and clear out with Joanna right away. Forfeit the rest of the tenancy.'

'Don't go,' said Owen.

'Why not?'

He didn't answer. He said slowly after a minute or two, 'After all—I dare say you're right. Lymstock isn't healthy just now. It might—it might harm you or—or your sister.'

'Nothing harms Joanna,' I said. 'She's tough. I'm the weakly one. Somehow this business makes me sick.'

'It makes *me* sick,' said Owen.

I pushed the door of the house agents half open.

'But I shan't go,' I said. 'Vulgar curiosity is stronger than pusillanimity. I want to know the solution.'

I went in.

A woman who was typing got up and came towards me. She had frizzy hair and simpered, but I found her more intelligent than the spectacled youth who had previously held sway in the outer office.

A minute or two later something familiar about her penetrated through to my consciousness. It was Miss Ginch, lately Symmington's lady clerk. I commented on the fact.

'You were with Galbraith and Symmington, weren't you?' I said.

'Yes. Yes, indeed. But I thought it was better to leave. This is quite a good post, though not quite so well paid. But there are things that are more valuable than money, don't you think so?'

'Undoubtedly,' I said.

'Those awful letters,' breathed Miss Ginch in a sibilant

99

whisper. 'I got a dreadful one. About me and Mr Symmington—oh, terrible it was, saying the most *awful* things! I knew my duty and I took it to the police, though of course it wasn't exactly *pleasant* for me, was it?'

'No, no, most unpleasant.'

'But they thanked me and said I had done quite right. But I felt that, after that, if people were talking—and evidently they *must* have been, or where did the writer get the idea from?—then I must avoid even the appearance of evil, though there has never been anything at all *wrong* between me and Mr Symmington.'

I felt rather embarrassed.

'No, no, of course not.'

'But people have such evil minds. Yes, alas, such evil minds!'

Nervously trying to avoid it, I nevertheless met her eye, and I made a most unpleasant discovery.

Miss Ginch was thoroughly enjoying herself.

Already once today I had come across someone who reacted pleasurably to anonymous letters. Inspector Graves's enthusiasm was professional. Miss Ginch's enjoyment I found merely suggestive and disgusting.

An idea flashed across my startled mind.

Had Miss Ginch written these letters herself?

CHAPTER 7

When I got home I found Mrs Dane Calthrop sitting talking to Joanna. She looked, I thought, grey and ill.

'This has been a terrible shock to me, Mr Burton,' she said. 'Poor thing, poor thing.'

'Yes,' I said. 'It's awful to think of someone being driven to the stage of taking their own life.'

'Oh, you mean Mrs Symmington?'

'Didn't you?'

Mrs Dane Calthrop shook her head.

'Of course one is sorry for her, but it would have been bound to happen anyway, wouldn't it?'

'Would it?' said Joanna dryly.

Mrs Dane Calthrop turned to her.

'Oh, I think so, dear. If suicide is your idea of escape from trouble then it doesn't very much matter what the trouble is. Whenever some very unpleasant shock had to be faced, she'd have done the same thing. What it really comes down to is that she was that kind of woman. Not that one would have guessed it. She always seemed to me a selfish rather stupid woman, with a good firm hold on life. Not the kind to panic, you would think—but I'm beginning to realize how little I really know anyone.'

'I'm still curious as to whom you meant when you said "Poor thing,"' I remarked.

She stared at me.

'The woman who wrote the letters, of course.'

'I don't think,' I said dryly, 'I shall waste sympathy on her.'

Mrs Dane Calthrop leaned forward. She laid a hand on my knee.

'But don't you realize—can't you *feel*? Use your imagination. Think how desperately, violently unhappy anyone must be to sit down and write these things. How lonely, how cut off from human kind. Poisoned through and through, with a dark stream of poison that finds its outlet in this way. That's why I feel so self-reproachful. Somebody in this town has been racked with that terrible unhappiness, and I've had no idea of it. I should have had. You can't interfere with actions—I never do. But that black inward unhappiness—like a septic arm physically, all black and swollen. If you could cut it and let the poison out it would flow away harmlessly. Yes, poor soul, poor soul.'

She got up to go.

I did not feel like agreeing with her. I had no sympathy for our anonymous letter writer whatsoever. But I did ask curiously:

'Have you any idea at all, Mrs Calthrop, who this woman is?'

She turned her fine perplexed eyes on me.

'Well, I can guess,' she said. 'But then I might be wrong, mightn't I?'

She went swiftly out through the door, popping her head back to ask:

'Do tell me, why have you never married, Mr Burton?'

In anyone else it would have been an impertinence, but with Mrs Dane Calthrop you felt that the idea had suddenly come into her head and she had really wanted to know.

'Shall we say,' I said, rallying, 'that I have never met the right woman?'

'We can say so,' said Mrs Dane Calthrop, 'but it wouldn't be a very good answer, because so many men have obviously married the wrong woman.'

This time she really departed.

Joanna said:

'You know I really do think she's mad. But I like her. The people in the village here are afraid of her.'

'So am I, a little.'

'Because you never know what's coming next?'

'Yes. And there's a careless brilliancy about her guesses.'

Joanna said slowly: 'Do you really think whoever wrote these letters is very unhappy?'

'I don't know what the damned hag is thinking or feeling! And I don't care. It's her victims I'm sorry for.'

It seems odd to me now that in our speculations about Poison Pen's frame of mind, we missed the most obvious one. Griffith had pictured her as possibly exultant. I had envisaged her as remorseful—appalled by the result of her handiwork. Mrs Dane Calthrop had seen her as suffering.

Yet the obvious, the inevitable reaction we did not consider—or perhaps I should say, I did not consider. That reaction was Fear.

For with the death of Mrs Symmington, the letters had passed out of one category into another. I don't know what the legal position was—Symmington knew, I suppose, but it was clear that with a death resulting, the position of the writer of the letters was much more serious. There could now be no question of passing it off as a joke if the identity of the writer was discovered. The police were active, a Scotland Yard expert called in. It was vital now for the anonymous author to remain anonymous.

And granted that Fear was the principal reaction, other things followed. Those possibilities also I was blind to. Yet surely they should have been obvious.

Joanna and I came down rather late to breakfast the next morning. That is to say, late by the standards of Lymstock. It was nine-thirty, an hour at which, in London, Joanna was just unclosing an eyelid, and mine would probably be still tight shut. However when Partridge had said 'Breakfast at half-past eight, or nine o'clock?' neither Joanna nor I had had the nerve to suggest a later hour.

To my annoyance, Aimée Griffith was standing on the door-step talking to Megan.

She gave tongue with her usual heartiness at the sight of us.

'Hallo, there, slackers! I've been up for hours.'

That, of course, was her own business. A doctor, no doubt, has to have early breakfast, and a dutiful sister is there to pour out his tea, or coffee. But it is no excuse for coming and butting in on one's more somnolent neighbours. Nine-thirty is not the time for a morning call.

Megan slipped back into the house and into the dining-room, where I gathered she had been interrupted in her breakfast.

'I said I wouldn't come in,' said Aimée Griffith—though why it is more of a merit to force people to come and speak to you on the doorstep, than to talk to them inside the house I do not know. 'I just wanted to ask Miss Burton if she'd any vegetables to spare for our Red Cross stall on the main road. If so, I'd get Owen to call for them in the car.'

'You're out and about very early,' I said.

'The early bird catches the worm,' said Aimée. 'You have a better chance of finding people in this time of day. I'm off to Mr Pye's next. Got to go over to Brenton this after-noon. Guides.'

'Your energy makes me quite tired,' I said, and at that moment the telephone rang and I retired to the back of the hall to answer it, leaving Joanna murmuring rather doubtfully something about rhubarb and French beans and exposing her ignorance of the vegetable garden.

'Yes?' I said into the telephone mouthpiece.

A confused noise of deep breathing came from the other end of the wire and a doubtful female voice said 'Oh!'

'Yes?' I said again encouragingly.

'Oh,' said the voice again, and then it inquired adenoidally, 'Is that—what I mean—is that Little Furze?'

'This is Little Furze.'

'Oh!' This was clearly a stock beginning to every

sentence. The voice inquired cautiously: 'Could I speak to Miss Partridge just a minute?'

'Certainly,' I said. 'Who shall I say?'

'Oh. Tell her it's Agnes, would you? Agnes Waddle.'

'Agnes Waddle?'

'That's right.'

Resisting the temptation to say, 'Donald Duck to you,' I put down the telephone receiver and called up the stairs to where I could hear the sound of Partridge's activities overheard.

'Partridge. Partridge.'

Partridge appeared at the head of the stairs, a long mop in one hand, and a look of 'What is it *now*?' clearly discernible behind her invariably respectful manner.

'Yes, sir?'

'Agnes Waddle wants to speak to you on the telephone.'

'I beg your pardon, sir?'

I raised my voice. 'Agnes Waddle.'

I have spelt the name as it presented itself to my mind. But I will now spell it as it was actually written.

'Agnes Woddell—whatever can she want now?'

Very much put out of countenance, Partridge relinquished her mop and rustled down the stairs, her print dress crackling with agitation.

I beat an unobtrusive retreat into the dining-room where Megan was wolfing down kidneys and bacon. Megan, unlike Aimée Griffith, was displaying no 'glorious morning face'. In fact she replied very gruffly to my morning salutations and continued to eat in silence.

I opened the morning paper and a minute or two later Joanna entered looking somewhat shattered.

'Whew!' she said. 'I'm so tired. And I think I've exposed my utter ignorance of what grows when. Aren't there runner beans this time of year?'

'August,' said Megan.

'Well, one has them any time in London,' said Joanna defensively.

'Tins, sweet fool,' I said. 'And cold storage on ships from the far-flung limits of empire.'

'Like ivory, apes and peacocks?' asked Joanna.

'Exactly.'

'I'd rather have peacocks,' said Joanna thoughtfully.

'I'd like a monkey of my own as a pet,' said Megan.

Meditatively peeling an orange, Joanna said:

'I wonder what it would feel like to be Aimée Griffith, all bursting with health and vigour and enjoyment of life. Do you think she's ever tired, or depressed, or—or wistful?'

I said I was quite certain Aimée Griffith was never wistful, and followed Megan out of the open French window on to the veranda.

Standing there, filling my pipe, I heard Partridge enter the dining-room from the hall and heard her voice say grimly:

'Can I speak to you a minute, miss?'

'Dear me,' I thought. 'I hope Partridge isn't going to give notice. Emily Barton will be very annoyed with us if so.'

Partridge went on: 'I must apologize, miss, for being rung up on the telephone. That is to say, the young person who did so should have known better. I have never been in the habit of using the telephone or of permitting my friends to ring me up on it, and I'm very sorry indeed that it should have occurred, and the master taking the call and everything.'

'Why, that's quite all right, Partridge,' said Joanna soothingly, 'why shouldn't your friends use the phone if they want to speak to you?'

Partridge's face, I could feel, though I could not see it, was more dour than ever as she replied coldly:

'It is not the kind of thing that has ever been done in this house. Miss Emily would never permit it. As I say, I am sorry it occurred, but Agnes Woddell, the girl who did it, was upset and she's young too, and doesn't know what's fitting in a gentleman's house.'

'That's one for you, Joanna,' I thought gleefully.

'This Agnes who rung me up, miss,' went on Partridge, 'she used to be in service here under me. Sixteen she was, then, and come straight from the orphanage. And you see, not having a home, or a mother or any relations to advise her, she's been in the habit of coming to me. I can tell her what's what, you see.'

'Yes?' said Joanna and waited. Clearly there was more to follow.

'So I am taking the liberty of asking you, miss, if you would allow Agnes to come here to tea this afternoon in the kitchen. It's her day out, you see, and she's got something on her mind she wants to consult me about. I wouldn't dream of suggesting such a thing in the usual way.'

Joanna said, bewildered:

'But why shouldn't you have anyone to tea with you?'

Partridge drew herself up at this, so Joanna said afterwards, and really looked most formidable, as she replied:

'It has never been the custom of This House, miss. Old Mrs Barton never allowed visitors in the kitchen, excepting as it should be our own day out, in which case we were allowed to entertain friends here instead of going out, but otherwise, on ordinary days, no. And Miss Emily she keeps to the old ways.'

Joanna is very nice to servants and most of them like her but she has never cut any ice with Partridge.

'It's no good, my girl,' I said when Partridge had gone and Joanna had joined me outside. 'Your sympathy and leniency are not appreciated. The good old overbearing ways for Partridge and things done the way they should be done in a gentleman's house.'

'I never heard of such tyranny as not allowing them to have their friends to see them,' said Joanna. 'It's all very well, Jerry, but they can't *like* being treated like slaves.'

'Evidently they do,' I said. 'At least the Partridges of this world do.'

'I can't imagine why she doesn't like me. Most people do.'

'She probably despises you as an inadequate housekeeper. You never draw your hand across a shelf and examine it for traces of dust. You don't look under the mats. You don't ask what happened to the remains of the chocolate soufflé, and you never order a nice bread pudding.'

'Ugh!' said Joanna.

She went on sadly. 'I'm a failure all round today. Despised by our Aimée for ignorance of the vegetable kingdom. Snubbed by Partridge for being a human being. I shall now go out into the garden and eat worms.'

'Megan's there already,' I said.

For Megan had wandered away a few minutes previously and was now standing aimlessly in the middle of a patch of lawn looking not unlike a meditative bird waiting for nourishment.

She came back, however, towards us and said abruptly:

'I say, I must go home today.'

'What?' I was dismayed.

She went on, flushing, but speaking with nervous determination.

'It's been awfully good of you having me and I expect I've been a fearful nuisance, but I have enjoyed it awfully, only now I must go back, because after all, well, it's my home and one can't stay away for ever, so I think I'll go this morning.'

Both Joanna and I tried to make her change her mind, but she was quite adamant, and finally Joanna got out the car and Megan went upstairs and came down a few minutes later with her belongings packed up again.

The only person pleased seemed to be Partridge, who had almost a smile on her grim face. She had never liked Megan much.

I was standing in the middle of the lawn when Joanna returned.

She asked me if I thought I was a sundial.

'Why?'

'Standing there like a garden ornament. Only one couldn't put on you the motto of only marking the sunny hours. You looked like thunder!'

'I'm out of humour. First Aimée Griffith—('Gracious!' murmured Joanna in parenthesis, 'I must speak about those vegetables!') and then Megan beetling off. I'd thought of taking her for a walk up to Legge Tor.'

'With a collar and lead, I suppose?' said Joanna.

'What?'

Joanna repeated loudly and clearly as she moved off round the corner of the house to the kitchen garden:

'I said, "With a collar and lead, I suppose?" Master's lost his dog, that's what's the matter with you!'

I was annoyed, I must confess, at the abrupt way in which Megan had left us. Perhaps she had suddenly got bored with us.

After all, it wasn't a very amusing life for a girl. At home she'd got the kids and Elsie Holland.

I heard Joanna returning and hastily moved in case she should make more rude remarks about sundials.

Owen Griffith called in his car just before lunch time, and the gardener was waiting for him with the necessary garden produce.

Whilst old Adams was stowing it in the car I brought Owen indoors for a drink. He wouldn't stay to lunch.

When I came in with the sherry I found Joanna had begun doing her stuff.

No signs of animosity now. She was curled up in the corner of the sofa and was positively purring, asking Owen questions about his work, if he liked being a G.P., if he wouldn't rather have specialized? She thought doctoring was one of the most fascinating things in the world.

Say what you will of her, Joanna is a lovely, a heaven-born listener. And after listening to so many would-be geniuses telling her how they had been unappreciated, listening to Owen Griffith was easy money. By the time we had got to the third glass of sherry, Griffith was telling her about some obscure reaction or lesion in such scientific terms that nobody could have understood a word of it except a fellow medico.

Joanna was looking intelligent and deeply interested.

I felt a moment's qualm. It was really too bad of Joanna. Griffith was too good a chap to be played fast and loose with. Women really were devils.

Then I caught a sideways view of Griffith, his long purposeful chin and the grim set of his lips, and I was not so sure that Joanna was going to have it her own way after all. And anyway, a man has no business to let himself be made a fool of by a woman. It's his own look-out if he does.

Then Joanna said:

'Do change your mind and stay to lunch with us, Dr Griffith,' and Griffith flushed a little and said he would, only his sister would be expecting him back—

'We'll ring her up and explain,' said Joanna quickly and went out into the hall and did so.

I thought Griffith looked a little uneasy, and it crossed my mind that he was probably a little afraid of his sister.

Joanna came back smiling and said that that was all right.

And Owen Griffith stayed to lunch and seemed to enjoy himself. We talked about books and plays and world politics, and about music and painting and modern architecture.

We didn't talk about Lymstock at all, or about anonymous letters, or Mrs Symmington's suicide.

We got right away from everything, and I think Owen Griffith was happy. His dark sad face lighted up, and he revealed an interesting mind.

When he had gone I said to Joanna:

'That fellow's too good for your tricks.'

Joanna said:

'That's what you say! You men all stick together!'

'Why were you out after his hide, Joanna? Wounded vanity?'

'Perhaps,' said my sister.

That afternoon we were to go to tea with Miss Emily Barton at her rooms in the village.

We strolled down there on foot, for I felt strong enough now to manage the hill back again.

We must actually have allowed too much time and got there early, for the door was opened to us by a tall rawboned fierce-looking woman who told us that Miss Barton wasn't in yet.

'But she's expecting you, I know, so if you'll come up and wait, please.'

This was evidently Faithful Florence.

We followed her up the stairs and she threw open a door and showed us into what was quite a comfortable sitting-room, though perhaps a little over-furnished. Some of the things, I suspected, had come from Little Furze.

The woman was clearly proud of her room.

'It's nice, isn't it?' she demanded.

'Very nice,' said Joanna warmly.

'I make her as comfortable as I can. Not that I can do for her as I'd like to and in the way she ought to have. She ought to be in her own house, properly, not turned out into rooms.'

Florence, who was clearly a dragon, looked from one to the other of us reproachfully. It was not, I felt, our lucky day. Joanna had been ticked off by Aimée Griffith and Partridge and now we were both being ticked off by the dragon Florence.

'Parlourmaid I was for fifteen years there,' she added.

Joanna, goaded by injustice, said:

'Well, Miss Barton wanted to let the house. She put it down at the house agents.'

'Forced to it,' said Florence. 'And she living so frugal and careful. But even then, the government can't leave her alone! Has to have its pound of flesh just the same.'

I shook my head sadly.

'Plenty of money there was in the old lady's time,' said Florence. 'And then they all died off one by one, poor dears. Miss Emily nursing of them one after the other. Wore herself out she did, and always so patient and uncomplaining. But it told on her, and then to have worry about money on top of it all! Shares not bringing in what they used to, so she says, and why not, I should like to know? They ought to be ashamed of themselves. Doing down a lady like her who's got no head for figures and can't be up to their tricks.'

'Practically everyone has been hit that way,' I said, but Florence remained unsoftened.

'It's all right for some as can look after themselves,

but not for *her*. She needs looking after, and as long as she's with me I'm going to see no one imposes on her or upsets her in any way. I'd do anything for Miss Emily.'

And glaring at us for some moments in order to drive that point thoroughly home, the indomitable Florence left the room, carefully shutting the door behind her.

'Do you feel like a blood-sucker, Jerry?' inquired Joanna. 'Because I do. What's the matter with us?'

'We don't seem to be going down very well,' I said. 'Megan gets tired of us, Partridge disapproves of you, faithful Florence disapproves of both of us.'

Joanna murmured, 'I wonder why Megan *did* leave?'

'She got bored.'

'I don't think she did at all. I wonder—do you think, Jerry, it could have been something that Aimée Griffith said?'

'You mean this morning, when they were talking on the doorstep.'

'Yes. There's wasn't much time, of course, but—'

I finished the sentence.

'But that woman's got the tread of a cow elephant! She might have—'

The door opened and Miss Emily came in. She was pink and a little out of breath and seemed excited. Her eyes were very blue and shining.

She chirruped at us in quite a distracted manner.

'Oh dear, I'm so sorry I'm late. Just doing a little shopping in the town, and the cakes at the Blue Rose didn't seem to me quite fresh, so I went on to Mrs Lygon's. I always like to get my cakes the last thing, then one gets the newest batch just out of the oven, and one isn't put off with the day before's. But I am so distressed to have kept you waiting—really unpardonable—'

Joanna cut in.

'It's our fault, Miss Barton. We're early. We walked down and Jerry strides along so fast now that we arrive everywhere too soon.'

'Never too soon, dear. Don't say that. One cannot have too much of a good thing, you know.'

And the old lady patted Joanna affectionately on the shoulder.

Joanna brightened up. At last, so it seemed, she was being a success. Emily Barton extended her smile to include me, but with a slight timidity in it, rather as one might approach a man-eating tiger guaranteed for the moment harmless.

'It's very good of you to come to such a feminine meal as tea, Mr Burton.'

Emily Barton, I think, has a mental picture of men as interminably consuming whiskies and sodas and smoking cigars, and in the intervals dropping out to do a few seductions of village maidens, or to conduct a liaison with a married woman.

When I said this to Joanna later, she replied that it was probably wishful thinking, that Emily Barton would have liked to come across such a man, but alas had never done so.

In the meantime Miss Emily was fussing round the room, arranging Joanna and myself with little tables, and carefully providing ashtrays, and a minute later the door opened and Florence came in bearing a tray of tea with some fine Crown Derby cups on it which I gathered Miss Emily had brought with her. The tea was china and delicious and there were plates of sandwiches and thin bread and butter, and a quantity of little cakes.

Florence was beaming now, and looked at Miss Emily with a kind of maternal pleasure, as at a favourite child enjoying a doll's tea party.

Joanna and I ate far more than we wanted to, our hostess pressed us so earnestly. The little lady was clearly enjoying her tea party and I perceived that, to Emily Barton, Joanna and I were a big adventure, two people from the mysterious world of London and sophistication.

Naturally, our talk soon dropped into local channels. Miss Barton spoke warmly of Dr Griffith, his kindness and his cleverness as a doctor. Mr Symmington, too, was a very clever lawyer, and had helped Miss Barton to get some money back from the income tax which she would never have known about. He was so nice to his children, too, devoted to them and to his wife—she caught herself up. 'Poor Mrs Symmington, it's so dreadfully sad, with those young children left motherless. Never, perhaps, a very strong woman—and her health had been bad of late. A brain storm, that is what it must have been. I read about such a thing in the paper. People really do not know what they are doing under those circumstances. And she can't have known what she was doing or else she would have remembered Mr Symmington and the children.'

'That anonymous letter must have shaken her up very badly,' said Joanna.

Miss Barton flushed. She said, with a tinge of reproof in her voice:

'Not a very nice thing to discuss, do you think, dear? I know there have been—er—letters, but we won't talk about them. Nasty things. I think they are better just ignored.'

Well, Miss Barton might be able to ignore them, but for some people it wasn't so easy. However I obediently changed the subject and we discussed Aimée Griffith.

'Wonderful, quite wonderful,' said Emily Barton. 'Her energy and her organizing powers are really splendid. She's so good with girls too. And she's so practical and up-to-date in every way. She really runs this place. And absolutely devoted to her brother. It's very nice to see such devotion between brother and sister.'

'Doesn't he ever find her a little overwhelming?' asked Joanna.

Emily Barton stared at her in a startled fashion.

'She has sacrificed a great deal for his sake,' she said with a touch of reproachful dignity.

I saw a touch of Oh Yeay! in Joanna's eye and hastened to divert the conversation to Mr Pye.

Emily Barton was a little dubious about Mr Pye.

All she could say was, repeated rather doubtfully, that he was very kind—yes, very kind. Very well off, too, and most generous. He had very strange visitors sometimes, but then, of course, he had travelled a lot.

We agreed that travel not only broadened the mind, but occasionally resulted in the forming of strange acquaintances.

'I have often wished, myself, to go on a cruise,' said

Emily Barton wistfully. 'One reads about them in the papers and they sound so attractive.'

'Why don't you go?' asked Joanna.

This turning of a dream into a reality seemed to alarm Miss Emily. 'Oh, no, no, that would be *quite* impossible.'

'But why? They're fairly cheap.'

'Oh, it's not only the expense. But I shouldn't like to go alone. Travelling alone would look very peculiar, don't you think?'

'No,' said Joanna.

Miss Emily looked at her doubtfully.

'And I don't know how I would manage about my luggage—and going ashore at foreign ports—and all the different currencies—'

Innumerable pitfalls seemed to rise up before the little lady's affrighted gaze, and Joanna hastened to calm her by a question about an approaching garden fête and sale of work. This led us quite naturally to Mrs Dane Calthrop.

A faint spasm showed for a minute on Miss Barton's face.

'You know, dear,' she said, 'she is really a very *odd* woman. The things she says sometimes.'

I asked what things.

'Oh, I don't know. Such very *unexpected* things. And the way she looks at you, as though you weren't there but somebody else was—I'm expressing it badly but it is so hard to convey the impression I mean. And then she won't— well, *interfere* at all. There are so many cases where a vicar's wife could advise and—perhaps *admonish*. Pull people up, you know, and make them mend their ways.

Because people would listen to her, I'm sure of that, they're all quite in awe of her. But she insists on being aloof and far away, and has such a curious habit of feeling sorry for the most unworthy people.'

'That's interesting,' I said, exchanging a quick glance with Joanna.

'Still, she is a very well-bred woman. She was a Miss Farroway of Bellpath, very good family, but these old families sometimes *are* a little peculiar, I believe. But she is devoted to her husband who is a man of very fine intellect—wasted, I am sometimes afraid, in this country circle. A good man, and most sincere, but I always find his habit of quoting Latin a little confusing.'

'Hear, hear,' I said fervently.

'Jerry had an expensive public school education, so he doesn't recognize Latin when he hears it,' said Joanna.

This led Miss Barton to a new topic.

'The schoolmistress here is a most unpleasant young woman,' she said. 'Quite *Red*, I'm afraid.' She lowered her voice over the word 'Red.'

Later, as we walked home up the hill, Joanna said to me:

'She's rather sweet.'

At dinner that night, Joanna said to Partridge that she hoped her tea-party had been a success.

Partridge got rather red in the face and held herself even more stiffly.

'Thank you, miss, but Agnes never turned up after all.'

'Oh, I'm sorry.'

'It didn't matter to *me*,' said Partridge.

She was so swelling with grievance that she condescended to pour it out to us.

'It wasn't me who thought of asking her! She rang up herself, said she'd something on her mind and could she come here, it being her day off. And I said, yes, subject to your permission which I obtained. And after that, not a sound or sign of her! And no word of apology either, though I should hope I'll get a postcard tomorrow morning. These girls nowadays—don't know their place—no idea of how to behave.'

Joanna attempted to soothe Partridge's wounded feelings.

'She mayn't have felt well. You didn't ring up to find out?'

Partridge drew herself up again.

'No, I did *not*, Miss. No, indeed. If Agnes likes to behave rudely that's her look-out, but I shall give her a piece of my mind when we meet.'

Partridge went out of the room still stiff with indignation and Joanna and I laughed.

'Probably a case of "Advice from Aunt Nancy's Column",' I said. '"*My boy is very cold in his manner to me, what shall I do about it?*" Failing Aunt Nancy, Partridge was to be applied to for advice, but instead there has been a reconciliation and I expect at this minute that Agnes and her boy are one of those speechless couples locked in each other's arms that you come upon suddenly standing by a dark hedge. They embarrass you horribly, but you don't embarrass them.'

Joanna laughed and said she expected that was it.

We began talking of the anonymous letters and wondered how Nash and the melancholy Graves were getting on.

'It's a week today exactly,' said Joanna, 'since Mrs Symmington's suicide. I should think they must have got on to something by now. Fingerprints, or handwriting, or *something*.'

I answered her absently. Somewhere behind my conscious mind, a queer uneasiness was growing. It was connected in some way with the phrase that Joanna had used, 'a week exactly'.

I ought, I dare say, to have put two and two together earlier. Perhaps, unconsciously, my mind was already suspicious.

Anyway the leaven was working now. The uneasiness was growing—coming to a head.

Joanna noticed suddenly that I wasn't listening to her spirited account of a village encounter.

'What's the matter, Jerry?'

I did not answer because my mind was busy piecing things together.

Mrs Symmington's suicide . . . She was alone in the house that afternoon . . . Alone in the house *because the maids were having their day out* . . . A week ago exactly . . .

'Jerry, what—'

I interrupted.

'Joanna, maids have days out once a week, don't they?'

'And alternate Sundays,' said Joanna. 'What on—'

'Never mind Sundays. They go out the same day every week?'

'Yes. That's the usual thing.'

Joanna was staring at me curiously. Her mind had not taken the track mine had done.

I crossed the room and rang the bell. Partridge came.

'Tell me,' I said, 'this Agnes Woddell. She's in service?'

'Yes, sir. At Mrs Symmington's. At Mr Symmington's, I should say now.'

I drew a deep breath. I glanced at the clock. It was half-past ten.

'Would she be back now, do you think?'

Partridge was looking disapproving.

'Yes, sir. The maids have to be in by ten there. They're old-fashioned.'

I said: 'I'm going to ring up.'

I went out to the hall. Joanna and Partridge followed me. Partridge was clearly furious. Joanna was puzzled. She said, as I was trying to get the number:

'What are you going to do, Jerry?'

'I'd like to be sure that the girl has come in all right.'

Partridge sniffed. Just sniffed, nothing more. But I did not care twopence about Partridge's sniffs.

Elsie Holland answered the telephone the other end.

'Sorry to ring you up,' I said. 'This is Jerry Burton speaking. Is—has—your maid Agnes come in?'

It was not until after I had said it that I suddenly felt a bit of a fool. For if the girl had come in and it was all right, how on earth was I going to explain my ringing up and asking. It would have been better if I had let Joanna ask the question, though even that would need a bit of explaining. I foresaw a new trail of gossip started in Lymstock, with myself and the unknown Agnes Woddell at its centre.

Elsie Holland sounded, not unnaturally, very much surprised.

'Agnes? Oh, she's sure to be in by now.'

I felt a fool, but I went on with it.

'Do you mind just seeing if she has come in, Miss Holland?'

There is one thing to be said for a nursery governess; she is used to doing things when told. Hers not to reason why! Elsie Holland put down the receiver and went off obediently.

Two minutes later I heard her voice.

'Are you there, Mr Burton?'

'Yes.'

'Agnes isn't in yet, as a matter of fact.'

I knew then that my hunch had been right.

I heard a noise of voices vaguely from the other end, then Symmington himself spoke.

'Hallo, Burton, what's the matter?'

'Your maid Agnes isn't back yet?'

'No. Miss Holland has just been to see. What's the matter? There's not been an accident, has there?'

'Not an *accident*,' I said.

'Do you mean you have reason to believe something has happened to the girl?'

I said grimly: 'I shouldn't be surprised.'

CHAPTER 8

I slept badly that night. I think that, even then, there were pieces of the puzzle floating about in my mind. I believe that if I had given my mind to it, I could have solved the whole thing then and there. Otherwise why did those fragments tag along so persistently?

How much do we know at any time? Much more, or so I believe, than we know we know! But we cannot break through to that subterranean knowledge. It is there, but we cannot reach it.

I lay on my bed, tossing uneasily, and only vague bits of the puzzle came to torture me.

There *was* a pattern, if only I could get hold of it. I ought to know who wrote those damned letters. There was a trail somewhere if only I could follow it . . .

As I dropped off to sleep, words danced irritatingly through my drowsy mind.

'No smoke without fire.' No fire without smoke. Smoke . . . Smoke? Smoke screen . . . No, that was the war—a war phrase. War. Scrap of paper . . . Only a scrap of paper. Belgium—Germany . . .

I fell asleep. I dreamt that I was taking Mrs Dane Calthrop, who had turned into a greyhound, for a walk with a collar and lead.

It was the ringing of the telephone that roused me. A persistent ringing.

I sat up in bed, glanced at my watch. It was half-past seven. I had not yet been called. The telephone was ringing in the hall downstairs.

I jumped out of bed, pulled on a dressing-gown, and raced down. I beat Partridge coming through the back door from the kitchen by a short head. I picked up the receiver.

'Hallo?'

'Oh—' It was a sob of relief. 'It's *you*!' Megan's voice. Megan's voice indescribably forlorn and frightened. 'Oh, please do come—*do* come. Oh, please do! Will you?'

'I'm coming at once,' I said. 'Do you hear? *At once.*'

I took the stairs two at a time and burst in on Joanna.

'Look here, Jo, I'm going off to the Symmingtons'.'

Joanna lifted a curly blonde head from the pillow and rubbed her eyes like a small child.

'Why—what's happened?'

'I don't know. It was the child—Megan. She sounded all in.'

'What do you think it is?'

'The girl Agnes, unless I'm very much mistaken.'

As I went out of the door, Joanna called after me:

'Wait. I'll get up and drive you down.'

'No need. I'll drive myself.'

'You can't drive the car.'

'Yes, I can.'

I did, too. It hurt, but not too much. I'd washed, shaved, dressed, got the car out and driven to the Symmingtons' in half an hour. Not bad going.

Megan must have been watching for me. She came out of the house at a run and clutched me. Her poor little face was white and twitching.

'Oh, you've come—you've *come*!'

'Hold up, funny face,' I said. 'Yes, I've come. Now what is it?'

She began to shake. I put my arm round her.

'I—I found her.'

'You found Agnes? Where?'

The trembling grew.

'Under the stairs. There's a cupboard there. It has fishing-rods and golf clubs and things. You know.'

I nodded. It was the usual cupboard.

Megan went on.

'She was there—all huddled up—and—and *cold*—horribly cold. She was—she was *dead*, you know!'

I asked curiously, 'What made you look there?'

'I—I don't know. You telephoned last night. And we all began wondering where Agnes was. We waited up some time, but she didn't come in, and at last we went to bed. I didn't sleep very well and I got up early. There was only Rose (the cook, you know) about. She was very cross about Agnes not having come back. She said she'd been before somewhere when a girl did a flit like that. I had some milk and bread and butter in the kitchen—and then suddenly Rose came in looking queer and she said that Agnes's outdoor things were still in her room. Her best ones that she goes out in. And I began to wonder if—if she'd ever left the house, and I started looking round, and I opened the cupboard under the stairs and—and she was there . . .'

'Somebody's rung up the police, I suppose?'

'Yes, they're here now. My stepfather rang them up straightaway. And then I—I felt I couldn't bear it, and I rang *you* up. You don't mind?'

'No,' I said. 'I don't mind.'

I looked at her curiously.

'Did anybody give you some brandy, or some coffee, or some tea after—after you found her?'

Megan shook her head.

I cursed the whole Symmington *ménage*. That stuffed shirt, Symmington, thought of nothing but the police. Neither Elsie Holland nor the cook seemed to have thought of the effect on the sensitive child who had made that gruesome discovery.

'Come on, slabface,' I said. 'We'll go to the kitchen.'

We went round the house to the back door and into the kitchen. Rose, a plump pudding-faced woman of forty, was drinking strong tea by the kitchen fire. She greeted us with a flow of talk and her hand to her heart.

She'd come all over queer, she told me, awful the palpitations were! Just think of it, it might have been *her*, it might have been any of them, murdered in their beds they might have been.

'Dish out a good strong cup of that tea for Miss Megan,'

I said. 'She's had a shock, you know. Remember it was she who found the body.'

The mere mention of a body nearly sent Rose off again, but I quelled her with a stern eye and she poured out a cup of inky fluid.

'There you are, young woman,' I said to Megan. 'You drink that down. You haven't got any brandy, I suppose, Rose?'

Rose said rather doubtfully that there was a drop of cooking brandy left over from the Christmas puddings.

'That'll do,' I said, and put a dollop of it into Megan's cup. I saw by Rose's eye that she thought it a good idea.

I told Megan to stay with Rose.

'I can trust you to look after Miss Megan?' I said, and Rose replied in a gratified way, 'Oh yes, sir.'

I went through into the house. If I knew Rose and her kind, she would soon find it necessary to keep her strength up with a little food, and that would be good for Megan too. Confound these people, why couldn't they look after the child?

Fuming inwardly I ran into Elsie Holland in the hall. She didn't seem surprised to see me. I suppose that the gruesome excitement of the discovery made one oblivious of who was coming and going. The constable, Bert Rundle, was by the front door.

Elsie Holland gasped out:

'Oh, Mr Burton, isn't it *awful*? Whoever can have done such a dreadful thing?'

'It *was* murder, then?'

'Oh, *yes*. She was struck on the back of the head. It's all blood and hair—oh! it's *awful*—and bundled into that cupboard. Who can have done such a wicked thing? And *why?* Poor Agnes, I'm sure she never did any one any harm.'

'No,' I said. 'Somebody saw to that pretty promptly.'

She stared at me. Not, I thought, a quick-witted girl. But she had good nerves. Her colour was, as usual, slightly heightened by excitement, and I even fancied that in a macabre kind of way, and in spite of a naturally kind heart, she was enjoying the drama.

She said apologetically: 'I must go up to the boys. Mr Symmington is so anxious that they shouldn't get a shock. He wants me to keep them right away.'

'Megan found the body, I hear,' I said. 'I hope somebody is looking after her?'

I will say for Elsie Holland that she looked conscience stricken.

'Oh dear,' she said. 'I forgot all about her. I do hope she's all right. I've been so rushed, you know, and the police and everything—but it was remiss of me. Poor girl, she must be feeling bad. I'll go and look for her at once.'

I relented.

'She's all right,' I said. 'Rose is looking after her. You get along to the kids.'

She thanked me with a flash of white tombstone teeth and hurried upstairs. After all, the boys were her job, and not Megan—Megan was nobody's job. Elsie was paid to look after Symmington's blinking brats. One could hardly blame her for doing so.

As she flashed round the corner of the stairs, I caught my breath. For a minute I caught a glimpse of a Winged

Victory, deathless and incredibly beautiful, instead of a conscientious nursery governess.

Then a door opened and Superintendent Nash stepped out into the hall with Symmington behind him.

'Oh, Mr Burton,' he said. 'I was just going to telephone you. I'm glad you are here.'

He didn't ask me—then—why I was here.

He turned his head and said to Symmington:

'I'll use this room if I may.'

It was a small morning-room with a window on the front of the house.

'Certainly, certainly.'

Symmington's poise was pretty good, but he looked desperately tired. Superintendent Nash said gently:

'I should have some breakfast if I were you, Mr Symmington. You and Miss Holland and Miss Megan will feel much better after coffee and eggs and bacon. Murder is a nasty business on an empty stomach.'

He spoke in a comfortable family doctor kind of way.

Symmington gave a faint attempt at a smile and said:

'Thank you, superintendent, I'll take your advice.'

I followed Nash into the little morning-room and he shut the door. He said then:

'You've got here very quickly? How did you hear?'

I told him that Megan had rung me up. I felt well disposed towards Superintendent Nash. He, at any rate, had not forgotten that Megan, too, would be in need of breakfast.

'I hear that you telephoned last night, Mr Burton, asking about this girl? Why was that?'

I suppose it did seem odd. I told him about Agnes's

telephone call to Partridge and her non-appearance. He said, 'Yes, I see . . .'

He said it slowly and reflectively, rubbing his chin.

Then he sighed:

'Well,' he said. 'It's murder now, right enough. Direct physical action. The question is, what did the girl know? Did she say anything to this Partridge? Anything definite?'

'I don't think so. But you can ask her.'

'Yes. I shall come up and see her when I've finished here.'

'What happened exactly?' I asked. 'Or don't you know yet?'

'Near enough. It was the maids' day out—'

'Both of them?'

'Yes, it seems that there used to be two sisters here who liked to go out together, so Mrs Symington arranged it that way. Then when these two came, she kept to the same arrangement. They used to leave cold supper laid out in the dining-room, and Miss Holland used to get tea.'

'I see.'

'It's pretty clear up to a point. The cook, Rose, comes from Nether Mickford, and in order to get there on her day out she has to catch the half-past two bus. So Agnes has to finish clearing up lunch always. Rose used to wash up the supper things in the evenings to even things up.

'That's what happened yesterday. Rose went off to catch the bus at two twenty-five, Symington left for his office at five-and-twenty to three. Elsie Holland and the children went out at a quarter to three. Megan Hunter went out on her bicycle about five minutes later. Agnes would then be alone in the house. As far as I can make out, she normally left the house between three o'clock and half-past three.'

'The house being then left empty?'

'Oh, they don't worry about that down here. There's not much locking up done in these parts. As I say, at ten minutes to three Agnes was alone in the house. That she never left it is clear, for she was in her cap and apron still when we found her body.'

'I suppose you can tell roughly the time of death?'

'Doctor Griffith won't commit himself. Between two o'clock and four-thirty, is his official medical verdict.'

'How was she killed?'

'She was first stunned by a blow on the back of the head. Afterwards an ordinary kitchen skewer, sharpened to a fine point, was thrust in the base of the skull, causing instantaneous death.'

I lit a cigarette. It was not a nice picture.

'Pretty cold blooded,' I said.

'Oh yes, yes, that was indicated.'

I inhaled deeply.

'Who did it?' I said. 'And why?'

'I don't suppose,' said Nash slowly, 'that we shall ever know exactly why. But we can guess.'

'She knew something?'

'She knew something.'

'She didn't give any one here a hint?'

'As far as I can make out, no. She's been upset, so the cook says, ever since Mrs Symmington's death, and according to this Rose, she's been getting more and more worried, and kept saying she didn't know what she ought to do.'

He gave a short exasperated sigh.

'It's always the way. They won't come to us. They've got that deep-seated prejudice against "being mixed up with the police". If she'd come along and told us what was worrying her, she'd be alive today.'

'Didn't she give the other woman *any* hint?'

'No, or so Rose says, and I'm inclined to believe her. For if she had, Rose would have blurted it out at once with a good many fancy embellishments of her own.'

'It's maddening,' I said, 'not to know.'

'We can still guess, Mr Burton. To begin with, it can't be anything very definite. It's got to be the sort of thing that you think over, and as you think it over, your uneasiness grows. You see what I mean?'

'Yes.'

'Actually, I think I know what it was.'

I looked at him with respect.

'That's good work, superintendent.'

'Well, you see, Mr Burton, I know something that you don't. On the afternoon that Mrs Symmington committed suicide both maids were supposed to be out. It was their day out. But actually Agnes came back to the house.'

'You know that?'

'Yes. Agnes has a boy friend—young Rendell from the fish shop. Wednesday is early closing and he comes along to meet Agnes and they go for a walk, or to the pictures if it's wet. That Wednesday they had a row practically as soon as they met. Our letter writer had been active, suggesting that Agnes had other fish to fry, and young Fred Rendell was all worked up. They quarrelled violently and

Agnes bolted back home and said she wasn't coming out unless Fred said he was sorry.'

'Well?'

'Well, Mr Burton, the kitchen faces the back of the house but the pantry looks out where we are looking now. There's only one entrance gate. You come through it and either up to the front door, or else along the path at the side of the house to the back door.'

He paused.

'Now I'll tell you something. That letter that came to Mrs Symmington that afternoon *didn't come by post*. It had a used stamp affixed to it, and the postmark faked quite convincingly in lamp-black, so that it would seem to have been delivered by the postman with the afternoon letters. But actually *it had not been through the post*. You see what that means?'

I said slowly: 'It means that it was left by *hand*, pushed through the letter box some time before the afternoon post was delivered, so that it should be amongst the other letters.'

'Exactly. The afternoon post comes round about a quarter to four. My theory is this. The girl was in the pantry looking through the window (it's masked by shrubs but you can see through them quite well) watching out for her young man to turn up and apologize.'

I said: '*And she saw whoever it was deliver that note?*'

'That's my guess, Mr Burton. I may be wrong, of course.'

'I don't think you are . . . It's simple—and convincing—and it means that Agnes knew *who the anonymous letter writer was*.'

'Yes.'

'But then why didn't she—?'

I paused, frowning.

Nash said quickly:

'As I see it, the girl *didn't realize what she had seen*. Not at first. Somebody had left a letter at the house, yes—but that somebody was nobody she would dream of connecting with the anonymous letters. It was somebody, from that point of view, quite above suspicion.

'But the more she thought about it, the more uneasy she grew. Ought she, perhaps, to tell someone about it? In her perplexity she thinks of Miss Barton's Partridge who, I gather, is a somewhat dominant personality and whose judgment Agnes would accept unhesitatingly. She decides to ask Partridge what she ought to do.'

'Yes,' I said thoughtfully. 'It fits well enough. And somehow or other, Poison Pen found out. How did she find out, superintendent?'

'You're not used to living in the country, Mr Burton. It's a kind of miracle how things get round. First of all there's the telephone call. Who overheard it your end?'

I reflected.

'I answered the telephone originally. Then I called up the stairs to Partridge.'

'Mentioning the girl's name?'

'Yes—yes, I did.'

'Any one overhear you?'

'My sister or Miss Griffith might have done so.'

'Ah, Miss Griffith. What was she doing up there?'

I explained.

'Was she going back to the village?'

'She was going to Mr Pye first.'

Superintendent Nash sighed.

'That's two ways it could have gone all over the place.'

I was incredulous.

'Do you mean that either Miss Griffith or Mr Pye would bother to repeat a meaningless little bit of information like that?'

'Anything's news in a place like this. You'd be surprised. If the dressmaker's mother has got a bad corn everybody hears about it! And then there is this end. Miss Holland, Rose—they could have heard what Agnes said. And there's Fred Rendell. It may have gone round through him that Agnes went back to the house that afternoon.'

I gave a slight shiver. I was looking out of the window. In front of me was a neat square of grass and a path and the low prim gate.

Someone had opened the gate, had walked very correctly and quietly up to the house, and had pushed a letter through the letter box. I saw, hazily, in my mind's eye, that vague woman's shape. The face was blank—but it must be a face that I knew . . .

Superintendent Nash was saying:

'All the same, this narrows things down. That's always the way we get 'em in the end. Steady, patient elimination. There aren't so very many people it could be now.'

'You mean—?'

'It knocks out any women clerks who were at their work all yesterday afternoon. It knocks out the school-mistress. She was teaching. And the district nurse. I know where she was yesterday. Not that I ever thought it was any of *them*, but now we're *sure*. You see, Mr Burton, we've got two definite times now on which to concentrate—yesterday afternoon, and the week before. On the day of Mrs Symmington's death from, say, a quarter-past three (the earliest possible time at which Agnes could have been back in the house after her quarrel) and four o'clock when the post must have come (but I can get that fixed more accurately with the postman). And yesterday from ten minutes to three (when Miss Megan Hunter left the house) until half-past three or more probably a quarter-past three as Agnes hadn't begun to change.'

'What do you think happened yesterday?'

Nash made a grimace.

'What do I think? I think a certain lady walked up to the front door and rang the bell, quite calm and smiling, the afternoon caller . . . Maybe she asked for Miss Holland, or for Miss Megan, or perhaps she had brought a parcel. Anyway Agnes turns round to get a salver for cards, or to take the parcel in, and our ladylike caller bats her on the back of her unsuspecting head.'

'What with?'

Nash said:

'The ladies round here usually carry large sizes in handbags. No saying what mightn't be inside it.'

'And then stabs her through the back of the neck and bundles her into the cupboard? Wouldn't that be a hefty job for a woman?'

Superintendent Nash looked at me with rather a queer expression.

'The woman we're after isn't normal—not by a long

way—and that type of mental instability goes with surprising strength. Agnes wasn't a big girl.'

He paused and then asked: 'What made Miss Megan Hunter think of looking in that cupboard?'

'Sheer instinct,' I said.

Then I asked: 'Why drag Agnes into the cupboard? What was the point?'

'The longer it was before the body was found, the more difficult it would be to fix the time of death accurately. If Miss Holland, for instance, fell over the body as soon as she came in, a doctor might be able to fix it within ten minutes or so—which might be awkward for our lady friend.'

I said, frowning:

'But if Agnes were suspicious of this person—'

Nash interrupted me.

'She wasn't. Not to the pitch of definite suspicion. She just thought it "queer". She was a slow-witted girl, I imagine, and she was only vaguely suspicious with a feeling that something was wrong. She certainly didn't suspect that she was up against a woman who would do murder.'

'Did you suspect that?' I asked.

Nash shook his head. He said, with feeling:

'I ought to have known. That suicide business, you see, frightened Poison Pen. She got the wind up. Fear, Mr Burton, is an incalculable thing.'

'Yes, fear. That was the thing we ought to have foreseen. Fear—in a lunatic brain . . .

'You see,' said Superintendent Nash, and somehow his words made the whole thing seem absolutely horrible.

'We're up against someone who's respected and thought highly of—someone, in fact, of good social position!'

Presently Nash said that he was going to interview Rose once more. I asked him, rather diffidently, if I might come too. Rather to my surprise he assented cordially.

'I'm very glad of your co-operation, Mr Burton, if I may say so.'

'That sounds suspicious,' I said. 'In books when a detective welcomes someone's assistance, that someone is usually the murderer.'

Nash laughed shortly. He said: 'You're hardly the type to write anonymous letters, Mr Burton.'

He added: 'Frankly, you can be useful to us.'

'I'm glad, but I don't see how.'

'You're a stranger down here, that's why. You've got no preconceived ideas about the people here. But at the same time, you've got the opportunity of getting to know things in what I may call a social way.'

'The murderer is a person of good social position,' I murmured.

'Exactly.'

'I'm to be the spy within the gates?'

'Have you any objection?'

I thought it over.

'No,' I said, 'frankly I haven't. If there's a dangerous lunatic about driving inoffensive women to suicide and hitting miserable little maidservants on the head, then I'm

140

not averse to doing a bit of dirty work to put that lunatic under restraint.'

'That's sensible of you, sir. And let me tell you, the person we're after is dangerous. She's about as dangerous as a rattlesnake and a cobra and a black mamba rolled into one.'

I gave a slight shiver. I said:

'In fact, we've got to make haste?'

'That's right. Don't think we're inactive in the force. We're not. We're working on several different lines.'

He said it grimly.

I had a vision of a fine far-flung spider's web . . .

Nash wanted to hear Rose's story again, so he explained to me, because she had already told him two different versions, and the more versions he got from her, the more likely it was that a few grains of truth might be incorporated.

We found Rose washing up breakfast, and she stopped at once and rolled her eyes and clutched her heart and explained again how she'd been coming over queer all the morning.

Nash was patient with her but firm. He'd been soothing the first time, so he told me, and peremptory the second, and he now employed a mixture of the two.

Rose enlarged pleasurably on the details of the past week, of how Agnes had gone about in deadly fear, and had shivered and said, 'Don't ask me,' when Rose had urged her to say what was the matter. 'It would be death if she told me,' that's what she said, finished Rose, rolling her eyes happily.

Had Agnes given no hint of what was troubling her?

No, except that she went in fear of her life.

Superintendent Nash sighed and abandoned the theme, contenting himself with extracting an exact account of Rose's own activities the preceding afternoon.

This, put baldly, was that Rose had caught the 2.30 bus and had spent the afternoon and evening with her family, returning by the 8.40 bus from Nether Mickford. The recital was complicated by the extraordinary presentiments of evil Rose had had all the afternoon and how her sister had commented on it and how she hadn't been able to touch a morsel of seed cake.

From the kitchen we went in search of Elsie Holland, who was superintending the children's lessons. As always, Elsie Holland was competent and obliging. She rose and said:

'Now, Colin, you and Brian will do these three sums and have the answers ready for me when I come back.'

She then led us into the night nursery. 'Will this do? I thought it would be better not to talk before the children.'

'Thank you, Miss Holland. Just tell me, once more, are you *quite* sure that Agnes never mentioned to you being worried over anything—since Mrs Symington's death, I mean?'

'No, she never said anything. She was a very quiet girl, you know, and didn't talk much.'

'A change from the other one, then!'

'Yes, Rose talks much too much. I have to tell her not to be impertinent sometimes.'

'Now, will you tell me exactly what happened yesterday afternoon? Everything you can remember.'

'Well, we had lunch as usual. One o'clock, and we hurry just a little. I don't let the boys dawdle. Let me see. Mr Symington went back to the office, and I helped Agnes by laying the table for supper—the boys ran out in the garden till I was ready to take them.'

'Where did you go?'

'Towards Combeacre, by the field path—the boys wanted to fish. I forgot their bait and had to go back for it.'

'What time was that?'

'Let me see, we started about twenty to three—or just after. Megan was coming but changed her mind. She was going out on her bicycle. She's got quite a craze for bicycling.'

'I mean what time was it when you went back for the bait? Did you go into the house?'

'No. I'd left it in the conservatory at the back. I don't know what time it was then—about ten minutes to three, perhaps.'

'Did you see Megan or Agnes?'

'Megan must have started, I think. No, I didn't see Agnes. I didn't see anyone.'

'And after that you went fishing?'

'Yes, we went along by the stream. We didn't catch anything. We hardly ever do, but the boys enjoy it. Brian got rather wet. I had to change his things when we got in.'

'You attend to tea on Wednesdays?'

'Yes. It's all ready in the drawing-room for Mr Symmington. I just make the tea when he comes in. The children and I have ours in the schoolroom—and Megan, of course. I have my own tea things and everything in the cupboard up there.'

'What time did you get in?'

'At ten minutes to five. I took the boys up and started to lay tea. Then when Mr Symmington came in at five I went down to make his but he said he would have it with us in the schoolroom. The boys were so pleased. We played Animal Grab afterwards. It seems so awful to think of now—with that poor girl in the cupboard all the time.'

'Would anybody go to that cupboard normally?'

'Oh no, it's only used for keeping junk. The hats and coats hang in the little cloakroom to the right of the front door as you come in. No one might have gone to the other cupboard for months.'

'I see. And you noticed nothing unusual, nothing abnormal at all when you came back?'

The blue eyes opened very wide.

'Oh no, inspector, nothing at all. Everything was just the same as usual. That's what was so awful about it.'

'And the week before?'

'You mean the day Mrs Symmington—'

'Yes.'

'Oh, that was terrible—terrible!'

'Yes, yes, I know. You were out all that afternoon also?'

'Oh yes, I always take the boys out in the afternoon—if it's fine enough. We do lessons in the morning. We went up on the moor, I remember—quite a long way. I was afraid I was late back because as I turned in at the gate I saw Mr Symmington coming from his office at the other end of the road, and I hadn't even put the kettle on, but it was just ten minutes to five.'

'You didn't go up to Mrs Symmington?'

'Oh no. I never did. She always rested after lunch. She had attacks of neuralgia—and they used to come on after meals. Dr Griffith had given her some cachets to take. She used to lie down and try to sleep.'

Nash said in a casual voice:

'So no one would take her up the post?'

'The afternoon post? No, I'd look in the letter box and put the letters on the hall table when I came in. But very often Mrs Symmington used to come down and get it herself. She didn't sleep all the afternoon. She was usually up again by four.'

'You didn't think anything was wrong because she wasn't up that afternoon?'

'Oh, no, I never dreamed of such a thing. Mr Symmington was hanging up his coat in the hall and I said, "Tea's not quite ready, but the kettle's nearly boiling," and he nodded and called out, "Mona, Mona!"—and then as Mrs Symmington didn't answer he went upstairs to her bedroom, and it must have been the most terrible shock to him. He called me and I came, and he said, "Keep the children away," and then he phoned Dr Griffith and we forgot all about the kettle and it burnt the bottom out! Oh dear, it *was* dreadful, and she'd been so happy and cheerful at lunch.'

Nash said abruptly: 'What is your own opinion of that letter she received, Miss Holland?'

Elsie Holland said indignantly:

'Oh, I think it was wicked—wicked!'

'Yes, yes, I don't mean that. Did you think it was true?'

Elsie Holland said firmly:

'No, indeed I don't. Mrs Symmington was very sensitive—very sensitive indeed. She had to take all sorts of things for her nerves. And she was very—well, *particular*.' Elsie flushed. 'Anything of that sort—*nasty*, I mean—would have given her a great shock.'

145

Nash was silent for a moment, then he asked:

'Have you had any of these letters, Miss Holland?'

'No. No, I haven't had any.'

'Are you sure? Please'—he lifted a hand—'don't answer in a hurry. They're not pleasant things to get, I know. And sometimes people don't like to admit they've had them. But it's very important in this case that we should know. We're quite aware that the statements in them are just a tissue of lies, so you needn't feel embarrassed.'

'But I haven't, superintendent. Really I haven't. Not anything of the kind.'

She was indignant, almost tearful, and her denials seemed genuine enough.

When she went back to the children, Nash stood looking out of the window.

'Well,' he said, 'that's that! She says she hasn't received any of these letters. And she sounds as though she's speaking the truth.'

'She did certainly. I'm sure she was.'

'H'm,' said Nash. 'Then what I want to know is, why the devil hasn't she?'

He went on rather impatiently, as I stared at him.

'She's a pretty girl, isn't she?'

'Rather more than pretty.'

'Exactly. As a matter of fact, she's uncommonly good looking. And she's young. In fact she's just the meat an anonymous letter writer would like. Then why has she been left out?'

I shook my head.

'It's interesting, you know. I must mention it to Graves.

He asked if we could tell him definitely of any one who hadn't had one.'

'She's the second person,' I said. 'There's Emily Barton, remember.'

Nash gave a faint chuckle.

'You shouldn't believe everything you're told, Mr Burton. Miss Barton had one all right—more than one.'

'How do you know?'

'That devoted dragon she's lodging with told me—her late parlourmaid or cook. Florence Elford. Very indignant she was about it. Would like to have the writer's blood.'

'Why did Miss Emily say she hadn't had any?'

'Delicacy. Their language isn't nice. Little Miss Barton has spent her life avoiding the coarse and unrefined.'

'What did the letters say?'

'The usual. Quite ludicrous in her case. And incidentally insinuated that she poisoned off her old mother and most of her sisters!'

I said incredulously:

'Do you mean to say there's really this dangerous lunatic going about and we can't spot her right away?'

'We'll spot her,' said Nash, and his voice was grim. 'She'll write just one letter too many.'

'But, my goodness, man, she won't go on writing these things—not now.'

He looked at me.

'Oh yes she will. You see, *she can't stop now*. It's a morbid craving. The letters will go on, make no mistake about that.'

CHAPTER 9

I went and found Megan before leaving the house. She was in the garden and seemed almost back to her usual self. She greeted me quite cheerfully.

I suggested that she should come back to us again for a while, but after a momentary hesitation she shook her head.

'It's nice of you—but I think I'll stay here. After all, it is—well, I suppose, it's my home. And I dare say I can help with the boys a bit.'

'Well,' I said, 'it's as you like.'

'Then I think I'll stay. I could—I could—'

'Yes?' I prompted.

'If—if anything awful happened, I could ring you up, couldn't I, and you'd come.'

I was touched. 'Of course. But what awful thing do you think might happen?'

'Oh, I don't know.' She looked vague. 'Things seem rather like that just now, don't they?'

'For God's sake,' I said. 'Don't go nosing out any more bodies! It's not good for you.'

She gave me a brief flash of a smile.

'No, it isn't. It made me feel awfully sick.'

I didn't much like leaving her there, but after all, as she had said, it was her home. And I fancied that now Elsie Holland would feel more responsible for her.

Nash and I went up together to Little Furze. Whilst I gave Joanna an account of the morning's doings, Nash tackled Partridge. He rejoined us looking discouraged.

'Not much help there. According to this woman, the girl only said she was worried about something and didn't know what to do and that she'd like Miss Partridge's advice.'

'Did Partridge mention the fact to any one?' asked Joanna.

Nash nodded, looking grim.

'Yes, she told Mrs Emory—your daily woman—on the lines, as far as I can gather, that there were *some* young women who were willing to take advice from their elders and didn't think they could settle everything for themselves off-hand! Agnes mightn't be very bright, but she was a nice respectful girl and knew her manners.'

'Partridge preening herself, in fact,' murmured Joanna. 'And Mrs Emory could have passed it round the town?'

'That's right, Miss Burton.'

'There's one thing rather surprises me,' I said. 'Why were my sister and I included among the recipients of the anonymous letters? We were strangers down here—nobody could have had a grudge against us.'

'You're failing to allow for the mentality of a Poison Pen—all is grist that comes to their mill. Their grudge, you might say, is against humanity.'

'I suppose,' said Joanna thoughtfully, 'that that is what Mrs Dane Calthrop meant.'

Nash looked at her inquiringly, but she did not enlighten him. The superintendent said:

'I don't know if you happened to look closely at the envelope of the letter you got, Miss Burton. If so, you may have noticed that it was actually addressed to Miss Barton, and the *a* altered to a *u* afterwards.'

That remark, properly interpreted, ought to have given us a clue to the whole business. As it was, none of us saw any significance in it.

Nash went off, and I was left with Joanna. She actually said: 'You don't think that letter can really have been meant for Miss Emily, do you?'

'It would hardly have begun "You painted trollop",' I pointed out, and Joanna agreed.

Then she suggested that I should go down to the town. 'You ought to hear what everyone is saying. It will be *the* topic this morning!'

I suggested that she should come too, but rather to my surprise Joanna refused. She said she was going to mess about in the garden.

I paused in the doorway and said, lowering my voice:

'I suppose Partridge is all right?'

'Partridge!'

The amazement in Joanna's voice made me feel ashamed of my idea. I said apologetically: 'I just wondered. She's rather "queer" in some ways—a grim spinster—the sort of person who might have religious mania.'

'This isn't religious mania—or so you told me Graves said.'

'Well, sex mania. They're very closely tied up together, I understand. She's repressed and respectable, and has been shut up here with a lot of elderly women for years.'

'What put the idea into your head?'

I said slowly:

'Well, we've only her word for it, haven't we, as to what the girl Agnes said to her? Suppose Agnes asked Partridge to tell her why Partridge came and left a note that day—and Partridge said she'd call round that afternoon and explain.'

'And then camouflaged it by coming to us and asking if the girl could come here?'

'Yes.'

'But Partridge never went out that afternoon.'

'We don't know that. We were out ourselves, remember.'

'Yes, that's true. It's possible, I suppose.' Joanna turned it over in her mind. 'But I don't think so, all the same. I don't think Partridge has the mentality to cover her tracks over the letters. To wipe off fingerprints, and all that. It isn't only cunning you want—it's knowledge. I don't think she's got that. I suppose—' Joanna hesitated, then said slowly, 'they are sure it is a woman, aren't they?'

'You don't think it's a man?' I exclaimed incredulously.

'Not—not an ordinary man—but a certain kind of man. I'm thinking, really, of Mr Pye.'

'So Pye is your selection?'

'Don't you feel yourself that he's a possibility? He's the sort of person who might be lonely—and unhappy—and spiteful. Everyone, you see, rather laughs at him. Can't you see him secretly hating all the normal happy people, and taking a queer perverse artistic pleasure in what he was doing?'

'Graves said a middle-aged spinster.'

'Mr Pye,' said Joanna, '*is* a middle-aged spinster.'

'A misfit,' I said slowly.

'Very much so. He's rich, but money doesn't help. And I do feel he might be unbalanced. He is, really, rather a *frightening* little man.'

'He got a letter himself, remember.'

'We don't know that,' Joanna pointed out. 'We only thought so. And anyway, he might have been putting on an act.'

'For our benefit?'

'Yes. He's clever enough to think of that—and not to overdo it.'

'He must be a first-class actor.'

'But of course, Jerry, whoever is doing this *must* be a first-class actor. That's partly where the pleasure comes in.'

'For God's sake, Joanna, don't speak so understandingly! You make me feel that you—that you understand the mentality.'

'I think I do. I can—just—get into the mood. If I weren't Joanna Burton, if I weren't young and reasonably attractive and able to have a good time, if I were—how shall I put it?—behind bars, watching other people enjoy life, would a black evil tide rise in me, making me want to hurt, to torture—even to destroy?'

'Joanna!' I took her by the shoulders and shook her. She gave a little sigh and shiver, and smiled at me.

'I frightened you, didn't I, Jerry? But I have a feeling

that that's the right way to solve this problem. You've got to be the person, knowing how they feel and what makes them act, and then—and then perhaps you'll know what they're going to do next.'

'Oh, hell!' I said. 'And I came down here to be a vegetable and get interested in all the dear little local scandals. Dear little local scandals! Libel, vilification, obscene language and murder!'

Joanna was quite right. The High Street was full of interested groups. I was determined to get everyone's reactions in turn.

I met Griffith first. He looked terribly ill and tired. So much so that I wondered. Murder is not, certainly, all in the day's work to a doctor, but his profession does equip him to face most things including suffering, the ugly side of human nature, and the fact of death.

'You look all in,' I said.

'Do I?' He was vague. 'Oh! I've had some worrying cases lately.'

'Including our lunatic at large?'

'That, certainly.' He looked away from me across the street. I saw a fine nerve twitching in his eyelid.

'You've no suspicions as to—*who*?'

'No. No. I wish to God I had.'

He asked abruptly after Joanna, and said, hesitatingly, that he had some photographs she'd wanted to see.

I offered to take them to her.

'Oh, it doesn't matter. I shall be passing that way actually later in the morning.'

I began to be afraid that Griffith had got it badly. Curse Joanna! Griffith was too good a man to be dangled as a scalp.

I let him go, for I saw his sister coming and I wanted, for once, to talk to her.

Aimée Griffith began, as it were, in the middle of a conversation.

'Absolutely shocking!' she boomed. 'I hear you were there—quite early?'

There was a question in the words, and her eyes glinted as she stressed the word 'early.' I wasn't going to tell her that Megan had rung me up. I said instead:

'You see, I was a bit uneasy last night. The girl was due to tea at our house and didn't turn up.'

'And so you feared the worst? Damned smart of you!'

'Yes,' I said. 'I'm quite the human bloodhound.'

'It's the first murder we've ever had in Lymstock. Excitement is terrific. Hope the police can handle it all right.'

'I shouldn't worry,' I said. 'They're an efficient body of men.'

'Can't even remember what the girl looked like, although I suppose she's opened the door to me dozens of times. Quiet, insignificant little thing. Knocked on the head and then stabbed through the back of the neck, so Owen tells me. Looks like a boy friend to me. What do you think?'

'That's your solution?'

'Seems the most likely one. Had a quarrel, I expect. They're very inbred round here—bad heredity, a lot of them.' She paused, and then went on, 'I hear Megan Hunter found the body? Must have given her a bit of a shock.'

I said shortly:

'It did.'

'Not too good for her, I should imagine. In my opinion she's not too strong in the head—and a thing like this might send her completely off her onion.'

I took a sudden resolution. I had to know something.

'Tell me, Miss Griffith, was it you who persuaded Megan to return home yesterday?'

'Well, I wouldn't say exactly persuaded.'

I stuck to my guns.

'But you did say something to her?'

Aimée Griffith planted her feet firmly and stared me in the eyes. She was, just slightly, on the defensive. She said:

'It's no good that young woman shirking her responsibilities. She's young and she doesn't know how tongues wag, so I felt it my duty to give her a hint.'

'Tongues—?' I broke off because I was too angry to go on.

Aimée Griffith continued with that maddeningly complacent confidence in herself which was her chief characteristic:

'Oh, I dare say *you* don't hear all the gossip that goes round. I do! I know what people are saying. Mind you, I don't for a minute think there's anything in it—not for a minute! But you know what people are—if they can say something ill-natured, they do! And it's rather hard lines on the girl when she's got her living to earn.'

'Her living to earn?' I said, puzzled.

Aimée went on:

'It's a difficult position for her, naturally. And I think she did the right thing. I mean, she couldn't go off at a moment's notice and leave the children with no one to look after them. She's been splendid—absolutely splendid. I say so to everybody! But there it is, it's an invidious position, and people will talk.'

'Who are you talking about?' I asked.

'Elsie Holland, of course,' said Aimée Griffith impatiently. 'In my opinion, she's a thoroughly nice girl, and has only been doing her duty.'

'And what are people saying?'

Aimée Griffith laughed. It was, I thought, rather an unpleasant laugh.

'They're saying that she's already considering the possibility of becoming Mrs Symmington No. 2—that she's all out to console the widower and make herself indispensable.'

'But, good God,' I said, shocked, 'Mrs Symmington's only been dead a week!'

Aimée Griffith shrugged her shoulders.

'Of course. It's absurd! But you know what people are! The Holland girl is young and she's good looking—that's enough. And mind you, being a nursery governess isn't much of a prospect for a girl. I wouldn't blame her if she wanted a settled home and a husband and was playing her cards accordingly.

'Of course,' she went on, 'poor Dick Symmington hasn't the least idea of all this! He's still completely knocked out by Mona Symmington's death. But you know what men are! If the girl is always there, making him comfortable, looking after him, being obviously devoted to the children—well, he gets to be dependent on her.'

I said quietly:

'So you do think that Elsie Holland is a designing hussy?'

Aimée Griffith flushed.

'Not at all. I'm sorry for the girl—with people saying nasty things! That's why I more or less told Megan that she ought to go home. It looks better than having Dick Symmington and the girl alone in the house.'

I began to understand things.

Aimée Griffith gave her jolly laugh.

'You're shocked, Mr Burton, at hearing what our gossiping little town thinks. I can tell you this—they always think the worst!'

She laughed and nodded and strode away.

I came upon Mr Pye by the church. He was talking to Emily Barton, who looked pink and excited.

Mr Pye greeted me with every evidence of delight.

'Ah, Burton, good morning, good morning! How is your charming sister?'

I told him that Joanna was well.

'But not joining our village parliament? We're all agog over the news. Murder! Real Sunday newspaper murder in our midst! Not the most interesting of crimes, I fear. Somewhat sordid. The brutal murder of a little serving maid. No finer points about the crime, but still undeniably, news.'

Miss Barton said tremulously:

Agatha Christie

'It is shocking—quite shocking.'

Mr Pye turned to her.

'But you enjoy it, dear lady, you enjoy it. Confess it now. You disapprove, you deplore, but there *is* the thrill. I insist, there *is* the thrill!'

'Such a nice girl,' said Emily Barton. 'She came to me from St Clotilde's Home. Quite a raw girl. But most teachable. She turned into such a nice little maid. Partridge was very pleased with her.'

I said quickly:

'She was coming to tea with Partridge yesterday afternoon.' I turned to Pye. 'I expect Aimée Griffith told you.'

My tone was quite casual. Pye responded apparently quite unsuspiciously: 'She did mention it, yes. She said, I remember, that it was something quite new for servants to ring up on their employers' telephones.'

'Partridge would never dream of doing such a thing,' said Miss Emily, 'and I am really surprised at Agnes doing so.'

'You are behind the times, dear lady,' said Mr Pye. 'My two terrors use the telephone constantly and smoked all over the house until I objected. But one daren't say too much. Prescott is a divine cook, though temperamental, and Mrs Prescott is an admirable house-parlourmaid.'

'Yes, indeed, we all think you're very lucky.'

I intervened, since I did not want the conversation to become purely domestic.

'The news of the murder has got round very quickly,' I said.

'Of course, of course,' said Mr Pye. 'The butcher, the

baker, the candlestick maker. Enter Rumour, painted full of tongues! Lymstock, alas! is going to the dogs. Anonymous letters, murders, any amount of criminal tendencies.'

Emily Barton said nervously: 'They don't think—there's no idea—that—that the two are connected.'

Mr Pye pounced on the idea.

'An interesting speculation. The girl knew something, therefore she was murdered. Yes, yes, most promising. How clever of you to think of it.'

'I—I can't bear it.'

Emily Barton spoke abruptly and turned away, walking very fast.

Pye looked after her. His cherubic face was pursed up quizzically.

He turned back to me and shook his head gently.

'A sensitive soul. A charming creature, don't you think? Absolutely a period piece. She's not, you know, of her own generation, she's of the generation before that. The mother must have been a woman of a very strong character. She kept the family time ticking at about 1870, I should say. The whole family preserved under a glass case. I do like to come across that sort of thing.'

I did not want to talk about period pieces.

'What do you really think about all this business?' I asked.

'Meaning by that?'

'Anonymous letters, murder . . .'

'Our local crime wave? What do you?'

'I asked you first,' I said pleasantly.

My Pye said gently:

'I'm a student, you know, of abnormalities. They interest me. Such apparently unlikely people do the most fantastic things. Take the case of Lizzie Borden. There's not really a reasonable explanation of that. In this case, my advice to the police would be—study *character*. Leave your fingerprints and your measuring of handwriting and your microscopes. Notice instead what people do with their hands, and their little tricks of manner, and the way they eat their food, and if they laugh sometimes for no apparent reason.'

I raised my eyebrows. 'Mad?' I said.

'Quite, quite mad,' said Mr Pye, and added, 'but you'd never know it!'

'Who?'

His eyes met mine. He smiled.

'No, no, Burton, that would be slander. We can't add slander to all the rest of it.'

He fairly skipped off down the street.

As I stood staring after him the church door opened and the Rev. Caleb Dane Calthrop came out.

He smiled vaguely at me.

'Good—good morning, Mr—er—er—'

I helped him. 'Burton.'

'Of course, of course, you mustn't think I don't remember you. Your name had just slipped my memory for the moment. A beautiful day.'

'Yes,' I said rather shortly.

He peered at me.

'But something—something—ah, yes, that poor unfortunate child who was in service at the Symmingtons'. I find it hard to believe, I must confess, that we have a murderer in our midst, Mr—er—Burton.'

'It does seem a bit fantastic,' I said.

'Something else has just reached my ears.' He leaned towards me. 'I learn that there have been anonymous letters going about. Have you heard any rumour of such things?'

'I have heard,' I said.

'Cowardly and dastardly things.' He paused and quoted an enormous stream of Latin. 'Those words of Horace are very applicable, don't you think?' he said.

'Absolutely,' I said.

There didn't seem anyone more I could profitably talk to, so I went home, dropping in for some tobacco and for a bottle of sherry, so as to get some of the humbler opinions on the crime.

'A narsty tramp,' seemed to be the verdict.

'Come to the door, they do, and whine and ask for money, and then if it's a girl alone in the house, they turn narsty. My sister Dora, over to Combeacre, she had a narsty experience one day—Drunk, he was, and selling those little printed poems . . .'

The story went on, ending with the intrepid Dora courageously banging the door in the man's face and taking refuge and barricading herself in some vague retreat, which I gathered from the delicacy in mentioning it must be the lavatory. 'And there she stayed till her lady came home!'

I reached Little Furze just a few minutes before lunch time. Joanna was standing in the drawing-room window doing nothing at all and looking as though her thoughts were miles away.

'What have you been doing with yourself?' I asked.

'Oh, I don't know. Nothing particular.'

I went out on the veranda. Two chairs were drawn up to an iron table and there were two empty sherry glasses. On another chair was an object at which I looked with bewilderment for some time.

'What on earth is this?'

'Oh,' said Joanna, 'I think it's a photograph of a diseased spleen or something. Dr Griffith seemed to think I'd be interested to see it.'

I looked at the photograph with some interest. Every man has his own ways of courting the female sex. I should not, myself, choose to do it with photographs of spleens, diseased or otherwise. Still no doubt Joanna had asked for it!

'It looks most unpleasant,' I said.

Joanna said it did, rather.

'How was Griffith?' I asked.

'He looked tired and very unhappy. I think he's got something on his mind.'

'A spleen that won't yield to treatment?'

'Don't be silly. I mean something real.'

'I should say the man's got *you* on his mind. I wish you'd lay off him, Joanna.'

'Oh, do shut up. I haven't done anything.'

'Women always say that.'

Joanna whirled angrily out of the room.

The diseased spleen was beginning to curl up in the sun. I took it by one corner and brought it into the drawing-room. I had no affection for it myself, but I presumed it was one of Griffith's treasures.

I stooped down and pulled out a heavy book from the bottom shelf of the bookcase in order to press the photograph flat again between its leaves. It was a ponderous volume of somebody's sermons.

The book came open in my hand in rather a surprising way. In another minute I saw why. *From the middle of it a number of pages had been neatly cut out.*

I stood staring at it. I looked at the title page. It had been published in 1840.

There could be no doubt at all. I was looking at the book from the pages of which the anonymous letters had been put together. Who had cut them out?

Well, to begin with, it could be Emily Barton herself. She was, perhaps, the obvious person to think of. Or it could have been Partridge.

But there were other possibilities. The pages could have been cut out by anyone who had been alone in this room, any visitor, for instance, who had sat there waiting for Miss Emily. Or even anyone who called on business.

No, that wasn't so likely. I had noticed that when, one day, a clerk from the bank had come to see me, Partridge had shown him into the little study at the back of the house. That was clearly the house routine.

A visitor, then? Someone 'of good social position'. Mr Pye? Aimée Griffith? Mrs Dane Calthrop?

The gong sounded and I went in to lunch. Afterwards, in the drawing-room I showed Joanna my find.

We discussed it from every aspect. Then I took it down to the police station.

They were elated at the find, and I was patted on the back for what was, after all, the sheerest piece of luck.

Graves was not there, but Nash was, and rang up the other man. They would test the book for fingerprints, though Nash was not hopeful of finding anything. I may say that he did not. There were mine, Partridge's and nobody else's, merely showing that Partridge dusted conscientiously.

Nash walked back with me up the hill. I asked how he was getting on. 'We're narrowing it down, Mr Burton. We've eliminated the people it couldn't be.'

'Ah,' I said. 'And who remains?'

'Miss Ginch. She was to meet a client at a house yesterday afternoon by appointment. The house was situated not far along the Combeacre Road, that's the road that goes past the Symmingtons'. She would have to pass the house both going and coming . . . the week before, the day the anonymous letter was delivered, and Mrs Symmington committed suicide, was her last day at Symmington's office. Mr Symmington thought at first she had not left the office at all that afternoon. He had Sir Henry Lushington with him all the afternoon and rang several times for Miss Ginch. I find, however, that she did leave the office between three and four. She went out to get some high denomination of stamp of which they had run short. The office boy could have gone, but Miss Ginch elected to go, saying she had a headache and would like the air. She was not gone long.'

'But long enough?'

'Yes, long enough to hurry along to the other end of the village, slip the letter in the box and hurry back. I must say, however, that I cannot find anybody who saw her near the Symmingtons' house.'

'Would they notice?'

'They might and they might not.'

'Who else is in your bag?'

Nash looked very straight ahead of him.

'You'll understand that we can't exclude anybody— anybody at all.'

'No,' I said. 'I see that.'

He said gravely: 'Miss Griffith went to Brenton for a meeting of Girl Guides yesterday. She arrived rather late.'

'You don't think—'

'No, I don't think. But I don't *know*. Miss Griffith seems an eminently sane healthy-minded woman—but I say, I don't *know*.'

'What about the previous week? Could she have slipped the letter in the box?'

'It's possible. She was shopping in the town that afternoon.' He paused. 'The same applies to Miss Emily Barton. She was out shopping early yesterday afternoon and she went for a walk to see some friends on the road past the Symmingtons' house the week before.'

I shook my head unbelievingly. Finding the cut book

in Little Furze was bound, I knew, to direct attention to the owner of that house, but when I remembered Miss Emily coming in yesterday so bright and happy and excited . . .

Damn it all—excited . . . Yes, excited—pink cheeks—shining eyes—surely not because—not because—

I said thickly: 'This business is bad for one! One sees things—one imagines things—'

'Yes, it isn't very pleasant to look upon the fellow creatures one meets as possible criminal lunatics.'

He paused for a moment, then went on:

'And there's Mr Pye—'

I said sharply: 'So you have considered him?'

Nash smiled.

'Oh, yes, we've considered him all right. A very curious character—not, I should say, a very nice character. He's got no alibi. He was in his garden, alone, on both occasions.'

'So you're not only suspecting women?'

'I don't think a man wrote the letters—in fact I'm sure of it—and so is Graves—always excepting our Mr Pye, that is to say, who's got an abnormally female streak in his character. But we've checked up on *everybody* for yesterday afternoon. That's a murder case, you see. *You're* all right,' he grinned, 'and so's your sister, and Mr Symmington didn't leave his office after he got there and Dr Griffith was on a round in the other direction, and I've checked upon his visits.'

He paused, smiled again, and said, 'You see, we *are* thorough.'

I said slowly, 'So your case is eliminated down to those

four—Miss Ginch, Mr Pye, Miss Griffith and little Miss Barton?'

'Oh, no, no, we've got a couple more—besides the vicar's lady.'

'You've thought of *her*?'

'We've thought of *everybody*, but Mrs Dane Calthrop is a little too openly mad, if you know what I mean. Still, she *could* have done it. She was in a wood watching birds yesterday afternoon—and the birds can't speak for her.'

He turned sharply as Owen Griffith came into the police station.

'Hallo, Nash. I heard you were round asking for me this morning. Anything important?'

'Inquest on Friday, if that suits you, Dr Griffith.'

'Right. Moresby and I are doing the P.M. tonight.'

Nash said:

'There's just one other thing, Dr Griffith. Mrs Symmington was taking some cachets, powders or something, that you prescribed for her—'

He paused. Owen Griffith said interrogatively:

'Yes?'

'Would an overdose of those cachets have been fatal?'

Griffith said dryly:

'Certainly not. Not unless she'd taken about twenty-five of them!'

'But you once warned her about exceeding the dose, so Miss Holland tells me.'

'Oh that, yes. Mrs Symmington was the sort of woman who would go and overdo anything she was given—fancy that to take twice as much would do her twice as much good, and you don't want anyone to overdo even phenacetin or aspirin—bad for the heart. And anyway there's absolutely no doubt about the cause of death. It was cyanide.'

'Oh, I know that—you don't get my meaning. I only thought that when committing suicide you'd prefer to take an overdose of a soporific rather than to feed yourself prussic acid.'

'Oh quite. On the other hand, prussic acid is more dramatic and is pretty certain to do the trick. With barbiturates, for instance, you can bring the victim round if only a short time has elapsed.'

'I see, thank you, Dr Griffith.'

Griffith departed, and I said goodbye to Nash. I went slowly up the hill home. Joanna was out—at least there was no sign of her, and there was an enigmatical memorandum scribbled on the telephone block presumably for the guidance of either Partridge or myself.

'If Dr Griffith rings up, I can't go on Tuesday, but could manage Wednesday or Thursday.'

I raised my eyebrows and went into the drawing-room. I sat down in the most comfortable armchair—(none of them were very comfortable, they tended to have straight backs and were reminiscent of the late Mrs Barton)—stretched out my legs and tried to think the whole thing out.

With sudden annoyance I remembered that Owen's arrival had interrupted my conversation with the inspector, and that he had just mentioned two other people as being possibilities.

I wondered who they were.

Partridge, perhaps, for one? After all, the cut book had been found in this house. And Agnes could have been struck down quite unsuspecting by her guide and mentor. No, you couldn't eliminate Partridge.

But who was the other?

Somebody, perhaps, that I didn't know? Mrs Cleat? The original local suspect?

I closed my eyes. I considered four people, strangely unlikely people, in turn. Gentle, frail little Emily Barton? What points were there actually against her? A starved life? Dominated and repressed from early childhood? Too many sacrifices asked of her? Her curious horror of discussing anything 'not quite nice'? Was that actually a sign of inner preoccupation with just these themes? Was I getting too horribly Freudian? I remembered a doctor once telling me that the mutterings of gentle maiden ladies when going off under an anaesthetic were a revelation. 'You wouldn't think they knew such words!'

Aimée Griffith?

Surely nothing repressed or 'inhibited' about her. Cheery, mannish, successful. A full, busy life. Yet Mrs Dane Calthrop had said, 'Poor thing!'

And there was something—something—some remembrance . . . Ah! I'd got it. Owen Griffith saying something like, 'We had an outbreak of anonymous letters up North where I had a practice.'

Had that been Aimée Griffith's work too? Surely rather a coincidence. Two outbreaks of the same thing.

Stop a minute, they'd tracked down the author of those. Griffith had said so. A schoolgirl.

Cold it was suddenly—must be a draught, from the window. I turned uncomfortably in my chair. Why did I suddenly feel so queer and upset?

Go on thinking . . . Aimée Griffith? Perhaps it was Aimée Griffith, *not* that other girl? And Aimée had come down here and started her tricks again. And that was why Owen Griffith was looking so unhappy and hag ridden. He suspected. Yes, he suspected . . .

Mr Pye? Not, somehow, a very nice little man. I could imagine him staging the whole business . . . laughing . . .

That telephone message on the telephone pad in the hall . . . why did I keep thinking of it? Griffith and Joanna—he was falling for her . . . No, that wasn't why the message worried me. It was something else . . .

My senses were swimming, sleep was very near. I repeated idiotically to myself, 'No smoke without fire. No smoke without fire . . . That's it . . . it all links up together . . .'

And then I was walking down the street with Megan and Elsie Holland passed. She was dressed as a bride, and people were murmuring:

'She's going to marry Dr Griffith at last. Of course they've been engaged secretly for years . . .'

There we were, in the church, and Dane Calthrop was reading the service in Latin.

And in the middle of it Mrs Dane Calthrop jumped up and cried energetically:

'It's got to be stopped, I tell you. It's got to be stopped!'

For a minute or two I didn't know whether I was asleep or awake. Then my brain cleared, and I realized I was in

the drawing-room of Little Furze and that Mrs Dane
Calthrop had just come through the window and was
standing in front of me saying with nervous violence:

'It has got to be *stopped*, I tell you.'

I jumped up. I said: 'I beg your pardon. I'm afraid I was
asleep. What did you say?'

Mrs Dane Calthrop beat one fist fiercely on the palm of
her other hand.

'It's got to be stopped. These letters! Murder! You can't
go on having poor innocent children like Agnes Woddell
killed!'

'You're quite right,' I said. 'But how do you propose to
set about it?'

Mrs Dane Calthrop said:

'We've got to do something!'

I smiled, perhaps in rather a superior fashion.

'And what do you suggest that we should do?'

'Get the whole thing cleared up! I said this wasn't a
wicked place. I was wrong. It is.'

I felt annoyed. I said, not too politely:

'Yes, my dear woman, but what are you going to *do*?'

Mrs Dane Calthrop said: 'Put a stop to it all, of course.'

'The police are doing their best.'

'If Agnes could be killed yesterday, their best isn't good
enough.'

'So you know better than they do?'

'Not at all. *I* don't know anything at all. That's why I'm
going to call in an expert.'

I shook my head.

'You can't do that. Scotland Yard will only take over on

a demand from the chief constable of the county. Actually they *have* sent Graves.'

'I don't mean *that* kind of an expert. I don't mean someone who knows about anonymous letters or even about murder. I mean someone who knows *people*. Don't you see? We want someone who knows a great deal about *wickedness*!'

It was a queer point of view. But it was, somehow, stimulating.

Before I could say anything more, Mrs Dane Calthrop nodded her head at me and said in a quick, confident tone:

'I'm going to see about it right away.'

And she went out of the window again.

CHAPTER 10

The next week, I think, was one of the queerest times I have ever passed through. It had an odd dream quality. Nothing seemed real.

The inquest on Agnes Woddell was held and the curious of Lymstock attended *en masse*. No new facts came to light and the only possible verdict was returned, 'Murder by person or persons unknown.'

So poor little Agnes Woddell, having had her hour of limelight, was duly buried in the quiet old churchyard and life in Lymstock went on as before.

No, that last statement is untrue. Not as before . . .

There was a half-scared, half-avid gleam in almost everybody's eye. Neighbour looked at neighbour. One thing had been brought out clearly at the inquest—it was most unlikely that any stranger had killed Agnes Woddell. No tramps nor unknown men had been noticed or reported in the district. Somewhere, then, in Lymstock, walking down the High Street, shopping, passing the time of day, was a person who had cracked a defenceless girl's skull and driven a sharp skewer home to her brain.

And no one knew who that person was.

As I say, the days went by in a kind of dream. I looked at everyone I met in a new light, the light of a possible murderer. It was not an agreeable sensation!

And in the evenings, with the curtain drawn, Joanna and I sat talking, talking, arguing, going over in turn all the various possibilities that still seemed so fantastic and incredible.

Joanna held firm to her theory of Mr Pye. I, after wavering a little, had gone back to my original suspect, Miss Ginch. But we went over the possible names again and again.

Mr Pye?

Miss Ginch?

Mrs Dane Calthrop?

Aimée Griffith?

Emily Barton?

Partridge?

And all the time, nervously, apprehensively, we waited for something to happen.

But nothing did happen. Nobody, so far as we knew, received any more letters. Nash made periodic appearances in the town but what he was doing and what traps the police were setting, I had no idea. Graves had gone again.

Emily Barton came to tea. Megan came to lunch. Owen Griffith went about his practice. We went and drank sherry with Mr Pye. And we went to tea at the vicarage.

I was glad to find Mrs Dane Calthrop displayed none of the militant ferocity she had shown on the occasion of our last meeting. I think she had forgotten all about it.

She seemed now principally concerned with the destruction of white butterflies so as to preserve cauliflower and cabbage plants.

Our afternoon at the vicarage was really one of the most peaceful we had spent. It was an attractive old house and had a big shabby comfortable drawing-room with faded rose cretonne. The Dane Calthrops had a guest staying with them, an amiable elderly lady who was knitting something with white fleecy wool. We had very good hot scones for tea, the vicar came in, and beamed placidly on us whilst he pursued his gentle erudite conversation. It was very pleasant.

I don't mean that we got away from the topic of the murder, because we didn't.

Miss Marple, the guest, was naturally thrilled by the subject. As she said apologetically: 'We have so little to talk about in the country!' She had made up her mind that the dead girl must have been just like her Edith.

'Such a nice little maid, and so willing, but sometimes just a *little* slow to take in things.'

Miss Marple also had a cousin whose niece's sister-in-law had had a great deal of annoyance and trouble over some anonymous letters, so the letters, also, were very interesting to the charming old lady.

'But tell me, dear,' she said to Mrs Dane Calthrop, 'what do the village people—I mean the townspeople—say? What do *they* think?'

'Mrs Cleat still, I suppose,' said Joanna.

'Oh no,' said Mrs Dane Calthrop. 'Not *now*.'

Miss Marple asked who Mrs Cleat was.

Joanna said she was the village witch.

'That's right, isn't it, Mrs Dane Calthrop?'

The vicar murmured a long Latin quotation about, I think, the evil power of witches, to which we all listened in respectful and uncomprehending silence.

'She's a very silly woman,' said his wife. 'Likes to show off. Goes out to gather herbs and things at the full of the moon and takes care that everybody in the place knows about it.'

'And silly girls go and consult her, I suppose?' said Miss Marple.

I saw the vicar getting ready to unload more Latin on us and I asked hastily: 'But why shouldn't people suspect her of the murder now? They thought the letters were her doing.'

Miss Marple said: 'Oh! But the girl was killed with a *skewer*, so I hear—(very unpleasant!). Well, naturally, that takes *all* suspicion away from this Mrs Cleat. Because, you see, she could ill-wish her, so that the girl would waste away and die from natural causes.'

'Strange how these old beliefs linger,' said the vicar. 'In early Christian times, local superstitions were wisely incorporated with Christian doctrines and their more unpleasant attributes gradually eliminated.'

'It isn't superstition we've got to deal with here,' said Mrs Dane Calthrop, 'but *facts*.'

'And very unpleasant facts,' I said.

'As you say, Mr Burton,' said Miss Marple. 'Now *you*— excuse me if I am being too personal—are a stranger here, and have a knowledge of the world and of various aspects of life. It seems to me that you ought to be able to find a solution to this distasteful problem.'

I smiled. 'The best solution I have had was a dream. In my dream it all fitted in and panned out beautifully. Unfortunately when I woke up the whole thing was nonsense!'

'How interesting, though. Do tell me how the nonsense went!'

'Oh, it all started with the silly phrase "No smoke without fire." People have been saying that *ad nauseam*. And then I got it mixed up with war terms. Smoke screens, scrap of paper, telephone messages—No, that was another dream.'

'And what was that dream?'

The old lady was so eager about it, that I felt sure she was a secret reader of Napoleon's Book of Dreams, which had been the great stand-by of my old nurse.

'Oh! only Elsie Holland—the Symmingtons' nursery governess, you know, was getting married to Dr Griffith and the vicar here was reading the service in Latin—("Very appropriate, dear," murmured Mrs Dane Calthrop to her spouse) and then Mrs Dane Calthrop got up and forbade the banns and said it had got to be stopped!

'But that part,' I added with a smile, 'was true. I woke up and found you standing over me saying it.'

'And I was quite right,' said Mrs Dane Calthrop—but quite mildly, I was glad to note.

'But where did a telephone message come in?' asked Miss Marple, crinkling her brows.

'I'm afraid I'm being rather stupid. That wasn't in the

dream. It was just before it. I came through the hall and noticed Joanna had written down a message to be given to someone if they rang up . . .'

Miss Marple leaned forward. There was a pink spot in each cheek. 'Will you think me *very* inquisitive and *very* rude if I ask just what that message was?' She cast a glance at Joanna. 'I *do* apologize, my dear.'

Joanna, however, was highly entertained.

'Oh, I don't mind,' she assured the old lady. 'I can't remember anything about it myself, but perhaps Jerry can. It must have been something quite trivial.'

Solemnly I repeated the message as best I could remember it, enormously tickled at the old lady's rapt attention.

I was afraid the actual words were going to disappoint her, but perhaps she had some sentimental idea of a romance, for she nodded her head and smiled and seemed pleased.

'I see,' she said. 'I thought it might be something like that.'

Mrs Dane Calthrop said sharply: 'Like what, Jane?'

'Something quite ordinary,' said Miss Marple.

She looked at me thoughtfully for a moment or two, then she said unexpectedly:

'I can see you are a very clever young man—but not quite enough confidence in yourself. You ought to have!'

Joanna gave a loud hoot.

'For goodness' sake don't encourage him to feel like that. He thinks quite enough of himself as it is.'

'Be quiet, Joanna,' I said. 'Miss Marple understands me.'

Miss Marple had resumed her fleecy knitting. 'You know,'

she observed pensively. 'To commit a successful murder must be very much like bringing off a conjuring trick.'

'The quickness of the hand deceives the eye?'

'Not only that. You've got to make people look at the wrong thing and in the wrong place—Misdirection, they call it, I believe.'

'Well,' I remarked. 'So far everybody seems to have looked in the wrong place for our lunatic at large.'

'I should be inclined, myself,' said Miss Marple, 'to look for somebody very sane.'

'Yes,' I said thoughtfully. 'That's what Nash said. I remember he stressed respectability too.'

'Yes,' agreed Miss Marple. 'That's *very* important.'

Well, we all seemed agreed.

I addressed Mrs Calthrop. 'Nash thinks,' I said, 'that there will be more anonymous letters. What do you think?'

She said slowly: 'There may be, I suppose.'

'If the police think that, there will have to be, no doubt,' said Miss Marple.

I went on doggedly to Mrs Dane Calthrop.

'Are you still sorry for the writer?'

She flushed. 'Why not?'

'I don't think I agree with you, dear,' said Miss Marple. 'Not in this case.'

I said hotly: 'They've driven one woman to suicide, and caused untold misery and heartburnings!'

'Have you had one, Miss Burton?' asked Miss Marple of Joanna.

Joanna gurgled, 'Oh yes! It said the most frightful things.'

'I'm afraid,' said Miss Marple, 'that the people who are young and pretty are apt to be singled out by the writer.'

'That's why I certainly think it's odd that Elsie Holland hasn't had any,' I said.

'Let me see,' said Miss Marple. 'Is that the Symmingtons' nursery governess—the one you dreamt about, Mr Burton?'

'Yes.'

'She's probably had one and won't say so,' said Joanna.

'No,' I said, 'I believe her. So does Nash.'

'Dear me,' said Miss Marple. 'Now that's *very* interesting. That's the most interesting thing I've heard yet.'

As we were going home Joanna told me that I ought not to have repeated what Nash said about letters coming.

'Why not?'

'Because Mrs Dane Calthrop might be It.'

'You don't really believe that!'

'I'm not sure. She's a queer woman.'

We began our discussion of probables all over again.

It was two nights later that I was coming back in the car from Exhampton. I had had dinner there and then started back and it was already dark before I got into Lymstock.

Something was wrong with the car lights, and after slowing up and switching on and off, I finally got out to see what I could do. I was some time fiddling, but I managed to fix them up finally.

The road was quite deserted. Nobody in Lymstock is about after dark. The first few houses were just ahead, amongst them the ugly gabled building of the Women's

Institute. It loomed up in the dim starlight and something impelled me to go and have a look at it. I don't know whether I had caught a faint glimpse of a stealthy figure flitting through the gate—if so, it must have been so indeterminate that it did not register in my conscious mind, but I did suddenly feel a kind of overweening curiosity about the place.

The gate was slightly ajar, and I pushed it open and walked in. A short path and four steps led up to the door.

I stood there a moment hesitating. What was I really doing there? I didn't know, and then, suddenly, just near at hand, I caught the sound of a rustle. It sounded like a woman's dress. I took a sharp turn and went round the corner of the building towards where the sound had come from.

I couldn't see anybody. I went on and again turned a corner. I was at the back of the house now and suddenly I saw, only two feet away from me, an open window.

I crept up to it and listened. I could hear nothing, but somehow or other I felt convinced that there was someone inside.

My back wasn't too good for acrobatics as yet, but I managed to hoist myself up and drop over the sill inside. I made rather a noise unfortunately.

I stood just inside the window listening. Then I walked forward, my hands outstretched. I heard then the faintest sound ahead of me to my right.

I had a torch in my pocket and I switched it on.

Immediately a low, sharp voice said: 'Put that out.'

I obeyed instantly, for in that brief second I had recognized Superintendent Nash.

I felt him take my arm and propel me through a door and into a passage. Here, where there was no window to betray our presence to anyone outside, he switched on a lamp and looked at me more in sorrow than in anger.

'You *would* have to butt in just that minute, Mr Burton.'

'Sorry,' I apologized. 'But I got a hunch that I was on to something.'

'And so you were probably. Did you see anyone?'

I hesitated. 'I'm not sure,' I said slowly. 'I've got a vague feeling I saw someone sneak in through the front gate but I didn't really *see* anyone. Then I heard a rustle round the side of the house.'

Nash nodded.

'That's right. Somebody came round the house before you. They hesitated by the window, then went on quickly— heard *you*, I expect.'

I apologized again. 'What's the big idea?' I asked.

Nash said:

'I'm banking on the fact that an anonymous letter writer can't stop writing letters. She may know it's dangerous, but she'll have to do it. It's like a craving for drink or drugs.'

I nodded.

'Now you see, Mr Burton, I fancy whoever it is will want to keep the letters looking the same as much as possible. She's got the cut-out pages of that book, and can go on using letters and words cut out of them. But the envelopes present a difficulty. She'll want to type them on the same machine. She can't risk using another typewriter or her own handwriting.'

'Do you really think she'll go on with the game?' I asked incredulously.

'Yes, I do. And I'll bet you anything you like she's full of confidence. They're always vain as hell, these people! Well, then, I figured out that whoever it was would come to the Institute after dark so as to get at the typewriter.'

'Miss Ginch,' I said.

'Maybe.'

'You don't know yet?'

'I don't *know*.'

'But you suspect?'

'Yes. But somebody's very cunning, Mr Burton. Somebody knows all the tricks of the game.'

I could imagine some of the network that Nash had spread abroad. I had no doubt that every letter written by a suspect and posted or left by hand was immediately inspected. Sooner or later the criminal would slip up, would grow careless.

For the third time I apologized for my zealous and unwanted presence.

'Oh well,' said Nash philosophically. 'It can't be helped. Better luck next time.'

I went out into the night. A dim figure was standing beside my car. To my astonishment I recognized Megan.

'Hallo!' she said. 'I thought this was your car. What have you been doing?'

'What are you doing is much more to the point?' I said.

'I'm out for a walk. I like walking at night. Nobody

stops you and says silly things, and I like the stars, and things smell better, and everyday things look all mysterious.'

'All of that I grant you freely,' I said. 'But only cats and witches walk in the dark. They'll wonder about you at home.'

'No, they won't. They never wonder where I am or what *I'm* doing.'

'How are you getting on?' I asked.

'All right, I suppose.'

'Miss Holland look after you and all that?'

'Elsie's all right. She can't help being a perfect fool.'

'Unkind—but probably true,' I said. 'Hop in and I'll drive you home.'

It was not quite true that Megan was never missed.

Symmington was standing on the doorstep as we drove up.

He peered towards us. 'Hallo, is Megan there?'

'Yes,' I said. 'I've brought her home.'

Symmington said sharply:

'You mustn't go off like this without telling us, Megan. Miss Holland has been quite worried about you.'

Megan muttered something and went past him into the house. Symmington sighed.

'A grown-up girl is a great responsibility with no mother to look after her. She's too old for school, I suppose.'

He looked towards me rather suspiciously.

'I suppose you took her for a drive?'

I thought it best to leave it like that.

CHAPTER 11

On the following day I went mad. Looking back on it, that is really the only explanation I can find.

I was due for my monthly visit to Marcus Kent . . . I went up by train. To my intense surprise Joanna elected to stay behind. As a rule she was eager to come and we usually stayed up for a couple of days.

This time, however, I proposed to return the same day by the evening train, but even so I was astonished at Joanna. She merely said enigmatically that she'd got plenty to do, and why spend hours in a nasty stuffy train when it was a lovely day in the country?

That, of course, was undeniable, but sounded very unlike Joanna.

She said she didn't want the car, so I was to drive it to the station and leave it parked there against my return.

The station of Lymstock is situated, for some obscure reason known to railway companies only, quite half a mile from Lymstock itself. Half-way along the road I overtook Megan shuffling along in an aimless manner. I pulled up.

'Hallo, what are you doing?'

'Just out for a walk.'

'But not what is called a good brisk walk, I gather. You were crawling along like a dispirited crab.'

'Well, I wasn't going anywhere particular.'

'Then you'd better come and see me off at the station.' I opened the door of the car and Megan jumped in.

'Where are you going?' she asked.

'London. To see my doctor.'

'Your back's not worse, is it?'

'No, it's practically all right again. I'm expecting him to be very pleased about it.'

Megan nodded.

We drew up at the station. I parked the car and went in and bought my ticket at the booking office. There were very few people on the platform and nobody I knew.

'You wouldn't like to lend me a penny, would you?' said Megan. 'Then I'd get a bit of chocolate out of the slot machine.'

'Here you are, baby,' I said, handing her the coin in question. 'Sure you wouldn't like some clear gums or some throat pastilles as well?'

'I like chocolate best,' said Megan without suspecting sarcasm.

She went off to the chocolate machine, and I looked after her with a feeling of mounting irritation.

She was wearing trodden over shoes, and coarse unattractive stockings and a particularly shapeless jumper and skirt. I don't know why all this should have infuriated me, but it did.

I said angrily as she came back:

'Why do you wear those disgusting stockings?'

Megan looked down at them, surprised.

'What's the matter with them?'

'Everything's the matter with them. They're loath-some. And why wear a pullover like a decayed cabbage?'

'It's all right, isn't it? I've had it for years.'

'So I should imagine. And why do you—'

At this minute the train came in and interrupted my angry lecture.

I got into an empty first-class carriage, let down the window and leaned out to continue the conversation.

Megan stood below me, her face upturned. She asked me why I was so cross.

'I'm not cross,' I said untruly. 'It just infuriates me to see you so slack, and not caring how you look.'

'I couldn't look nice, anyway, so what does it matter?'

'My God,' I said. 'I'd like to see you turned out properly. I'd like to take you to London and outfit you from tip to toe.'

'I wish you could,' said Megan.

The train began to move. I looked down into Megan's upturned, wistful face.

And then, as I have said, madness came upon me.

I opened the door, grabbed Megan with one arm and fairly hauled her into the carriage.

There was an outraged shout from a porter, but all he could do was dexterously to bang shut the door again. I pulled Megan up from the floor where my impetuous action had landed her.

'What on earth did you do that for?' she demanded, rubbing one knee.

'Shut up,' I said. 'You're coming to London with me and when I've done with you you won't know yourself. I'll show you what you can look like if you try. I'm tired of seeing you mooch about down at heel and all anyhow.'

'Oh!' said Megan in an ecstatic whisper.

The ticket collector came along and I bought Megan a return ticket. She sat in her corner looking at me in a kind of awed respect.

'I say,' she said when the man had gone. 'You are sudden, aren't you?'

'Very,' I said. 'It runs in our family.'

How to explain to Megan the impulse that had come over me? She had looked like a wistful dog being left behind. She now had on her face the incredulous pleasure of the dog who has been taken on the walk after all.

'I suppose you don't know London very well?' I said to Megan.

'Yes, I do,' said Megan. 'I always went through it to school. And I've been to the dentist there and to a pantomime.'

'This,' I said darkly, 'will be a different London.'

We arrived with half an hour to spare before my appointment in Harley Street.

I took a taxi and we drove straight to Mirotin, Joanna's dressmaker. Mirotin is, in the flesh, an unconventional and breezy woman of forty-five, Mary Grey. She is a clever woman and very good company. I have always liked her.

I said to Megan. 'You're my cousin.'

'Why?'

'Don't argue,' I said.

Mary Grey was being firm with a stout woman who was enamoured of a skin-tight powder-blue evening dress. I detached her and took her aside.

'Listen,' I said. 'I've brought a little cousin of mine along. Joanna was coming up but was prevented. But she said I could leave it all to you. You see what the girl looks like now?'

'My God, I do,' said Mary Grey with feeling.

'Well, I want her turned out right in every particular from head to foot. *Carte blanche*. Stockings, shoes, undies, everything! By the way, the man who does Joanna's hair is close round here, isn't he?'

'Antoine? Round the corner. I'll see to that too.'

'You're a woman in a thousand.'

'Oh, I shall enjoy it—apart from the money—and that's not to be sneezed at in these days—half my damned brutes of women never pay their bills. But as I say, I shall enjoy it.' She shot a quick professional glance at Megan standing a little way away. 'She's got a lovely figure.'

'You must have X-ray eyes,' I said. 'She looks completely shapeless to me.'

Mary Grey laughed.

'It's these schools,' she said. 'They seem to take a pride in turning out girls who preen themselves on looking like nothing on earth. They call it being sweet and unsophisticated. Sometimes it takes a whole season before a girl can pull herself together and look human. Don't worry, leave it all to me.'

'Right,' I said. 'I'll come back and fetch her about six.'

*

Marcus Kent was pleased with me. He told me that I surpassed his wildest expectations.

'You must have the constitution of an elephant,' he said, 'to make a come-back like this. Oh well, wonderful what country air and no late hours or excitements will do for a man if he can only stick it.'

'I grant you your first two,' I said. 'But don't think that the country is free from excitements. We've had a good deal in my part.'

'What sort of excitement?'

'Murder,' I said.

Marcus Kent pursed up his mouth and whistled.

'Some bucolic love tragedy? Farmer lad kills his lass?'

'Not at all. A crafty, determined lunatic killer.'

'I haven't read anything about it. When did they lay him by the heels?'

'They haven't, and it's a she!'

'Whew! I'm not sure that Lymstock's quite the right place for you, old boy.'

I said firmly:

'Yes, it is. And you're not going to get me out of it.'

Marcus Kent has a low mind. He said at once:

'So that's it! Found a blonde?'

'Not at all,' I said, with a guilty thought of Elsie Holland. 'It's merely that the psychology of crime interests me a good deal.'

'Oh, all right. It certainly hasn't done you any harm so far, but just make sure that your lunatic killer doesn't obliterate *you*.'

'No fear of that,' I said.

190

'What about dining with me this evening? You can tell me all about your revolting murder.'

'Sorry. I'm booked.'

'Date with a lady—eh? Yes, you're definitely on the mend.'

'I suppose you could call it that,' I said, rather tickled at the idea of Megan in the role.

I was at Mirotin's at six o'clock when the establishment was officially closing. Mary Grey came to meet me at the top of the stairs outside the showroom. She had a finger to her lips.

'You're going to have a shock! If I say it myself, I've put in a good bit of work.'

I went into the big showroom. Megan was standing looking at herself in a long mirror. I give you my word I hardly recognized her! For the minute it took my breath away. Tall and slim as a willow with delicate ankles and feet shown off by sheer silk stockings and well-cut shoes. Yes, lovely feet and hands, small bones—quality and distinction in every line of her. Her hair had been trimmed and shaped to her head and it was glowing like a glossy chestnut. They'd had the sense to leave her face alone. She was not made up, or if she was it was so light and delicate that it did not show. Her mouth needed no lipstick.

Moreover there was about her something that I had never seen before, a new innocent pride in the arch of her neck. She looked at me gravely with a small shy smile.

'I do look—rather nice, don't I?' said Megan.

'Nice?' I said. 'Nice isn't the word! Come on out to dinner and if every second man doesn't turn round to look at you I'll be surprised. You'll knock all the other girls into a cocked hat.'

Megan was not beautiful, but she was unusual and striking looking. She had personality. She walked into the restaurant ahead of me and, as the head waiter hurried towards us, I felt the thrill of idiotic pride that a man feels when he has got something out of the ordinary with him.

We had cocktails first and lingered over them. Then we dined. And later we danced. Megan was keen to dance and I didn't want to disappoint her, but for some reason or other I hadn't thought she would dance well. But she did. She was light as a feather in my arms, and her body and feet followed the rhythm perfectly.

'Gosh!' I said. 'You can dance!'

She seemed a little surprised. 'Well, of course I can. We had dancing class every week at school.'

'It takes more than dancing class to make a dancer,' I said.

We went back to our table.

'Isn't this food lovely?' said Megan. 'And everything!'

She heaved a delighted sigh.

'Exactly my sentiments,' I said.

It was a delirious evening. I was still mad. Megan brought me down to earth when she said doubtfully:

'Oughtn't we to be going home?'

My jaw dropped. Yes, definitely I was mad. I had forgotten everything! I was in a world divorced from reality, existing in it with the creature I had created.

'Good Lord!' I said.

I realized that the last train had gone.

'Stay there,' I said. 'I'm going to telephone.'

I rang up the Llewellyn Hire people and ordered their biggest and fastest car to come round as soon as possible.

I came back to Megan. 'The last train has gone,' I said. 'So we're going home by car.'

'Are we? What fun!'

What a nice child she was, I thought. So pleased with everything, so unquestioning, accepting all my suggestions without fuss or bother.

The car came, and it was large and fast, but all the same it was very late when we came into Lymstock.

Suddenly conscience-stricken, I said, 'They'll have been sending out search parties for you!'

But Megan seemed in an equable mood. She said vaguely:

'Oh, I don't think so. I often go out and don't come home for lunch.'

'Yes, my dear child, but you've been out for tea and dinner too.'

However, Megan's lucky star was in the ascendant. The house was dark and silent. On Megan's advice, we went round to the back and threw stones at Rose's window.

In due course Rose looked out and with many suppressed exclamations and palpitations came down to let us in.

'Well now, and I saying you were asleep in your bed. The master and Miss Holland'—(slight sniff after Miss Holland's name)—'had early supper and went for a drive. I said I'd keep an eye to the boys. I thought I heard you come in when I was up in the nursery trying to quiet Colin, who was playing up, but you weren't about when I came down so I thought you'd gone to bed. And that's what I said when the master came in and asked for you.'

I cut short the conversation by remarking that that was where Megan had better go now.

'Good night,' said Megan, 'and thank you *awfully*. It's been the loveliest day I've ever had.'

I drove home slightly light-headed still, and tipped the chauffeur handsomely, offering him a bed if he liked. But he preferred to drive back through the night.

The hall door had opened during our colloquy and as he drove away it was flung wide open and Joanna said:

'So it's you at last, is it?'

'Were you worried about me?' I asked, coming in and shutting the door.

Joanna went into the drawing-room and I followed her. There was a coffee pot on the trivet and Joanna made herself coffee whilst I helped myself to a whisky and soda.

'Worried about you? No, of course not. I thought you'd decided to stay in town and have a binge.'

'I've had a binge—of a kind.'

I grinned and then began to laugh.

Joanna asked what I was laughing at and I told her.

'But Jerry, you must have been mad—quite mad!'

'I suppose I was.'

'But, my dear boy, you can't do things like that—not in a place like this. It will be all round Lymstock tomorrow.'

'I suppose it will. But, after all, Megan's only a child.'

'She isn't. She's twenty. You can't take a girl of twenty to London and buy her clothes without a most frightful scandal. Good gracious, Jerry, you'll probably have to marry the girl.'

Joanna was half-serious, half-laughing.

It was at that moment that I made a very important discovery. 'Damn it all,' I said. 'I don't mind if I do. In fact—I should like it.'

A very funny expression came over Joanna's face. She got up and said dryly, as she went towards the door:

'Yes, I've known that for some time . . .'

She left me standing, glass in hand, aghast at my new discovery.

CHAPTER 12

I don't know what the usual reactions are of a man who goes to propose marriage.

In fiction his throat is dry and his collar feels too tight and he is in a pitiable state of nervousness.

I didn't feel at all like that. Having thought of a good idea I just wanted to get it all settled as soon as possible. I didn't see any particular need for embarrassment.

I went along to the Symmingtons' house about eleven o'clock. I rang the bell and when Rose came, I asked for Miss Megan. It was the knowing look that Rose gave me that first made me feel slightly shy.

She put me in the little morning-room and whilst waiting there I hoped uneasily that they hadn't been upsetting Megan.

When the door opened and I wheeled round, I was instantly relieved. Megan was not looking shy or upset at all. Her head was still like a glossy chestnut, and she wore that air of pride and self-respect that she had acquired yesterday. She was in her old clothes again but she had managed to make them look different. It's wonderful what knowledge of her own attractiveness will do for a girl. Megan, I realized suddenly, had grown up.

I suppose I must really have been rather nervous, otherwise I should not have opened the conversation by saying affectionately, 'Hallo, catfish!' It was hardly, in the circumstances, a lover-like greeting.

It seemed to suit Megan. She grinned and said, 'Hallo!'

'Look here,' I said. 'You didn't get into a row about yesterday, I hope?'

Megan said with assurance, 'Oh, *no*,' and then blinked, and said vaguely, 'Yes, I believe I did. I mean, they said a lot of things and seemed to think it had been very odd—but then you know what people are and what fusses they make all about nothing.'

I was relieved to find that shocked disapproval had slipped off Megan like water off a duck's back.

'I came round this morning,' I said, 'because I've a suggestion to make. You see I like you a lot, and I think you like me—'

'Frightfully,' said Megan with rather disquieting enthusiasm.

'And we get on awfully well together, so I think it would be a good idea if we got married.'

'Oh,' said Megan.

She looked surprised. Just that. Not startled. Not shocked. Just mildly surprised.

'You mean you really want to marry me?' she asked with the air of one getting a thing perfectly clear.

'More than anything in the world,' I said—and I meant it.

'You mean, you're in love with me?'

'I'm in love with you.'

Her eyes were steady and grave. She said:

'I think you're the nicest person in the world—but I'm not in love with you.'

'I'll make you love me.'

'That wouldn't do. I don't want to be *made*.'

She paused and then said gravely: 'I'm not the sort of wife for you. I'm better at hating than at loving.'

She said it with a queer intensity.

I said, 'Hate doesn't last. Love does.'

'Is that true?'

'It's what I believe.'

Again there was a silence. Then I said:

'So it's "No," is it?'

'Yes, it's no.'

'And you don't encourage me to hope?'

'What would be the good of that?'

'None whatever,' I agreed, 'quite redundant, in fact—because I'm going to hope whether you tell me to or not.'

Well, that was that. I walked away from the house feeling slightly dazed but irritatingly conscious of Rose's passionately interested gaze following me.

Rose had had a good deal to say before I could escape.

That she'd never felt the same since that awful day! That she wouldn't have stayed except for the children and being sorry for poor Mr Symmington. That she wasn't going to stay unless they got another maid quick—and they wouldn't be likely to do that when there had been a murder in the house! That it was all very well for that Miss Holland to say she'd do the housework in the meantime. Very sweet and obliging she was—Oh yes, but it was mistress of the house that she was fancying herself going to be one fine day! Mr Symmington, poor man, never saw anything—but one knew what a widower was, a poor helpless creature made to be the prey of a designing woman. And that it wouldn't be for want of trying if Miss Holland didn't step into the dead mistress's shoes!

I assented mechanically to everything, yearning to get away and unable to do so because Rose was holding firmly on to my hat whilst she indulged in her flood of spite.

I wondered if there was any truth in what she said. Had Elsie Holland envisaged the possibility of becoming the second Mrs Symmington? Or was she just a decent kind-hearted girl doing her best to look after a bereaved household?

The result would quite likely be the same in either case. And why not? Symmington's young children needed a mother—Elsie was a decent soul—beside being quite indecently beautiful—a point which a man might appreciate—even such a stuffed fish as Symmington!

I thought all this, I know, because I was trying to put off thinking about Megan.

You may say that I had gone to ask Megan to marry me in an absurdly complacent frame of mind and that I deserved what I got—but it was not really like that. It was because I felt so assured, so certain, that Megan belonged to me—that she was my business, that to look after her and make her happy and keep her from harm was the only natural right way of life for me, that I had expected her to feel, too, that she and I belonged to each other.

But I was not giving up. Oh no! Megan was my woman and I was going to have her.

After a moment's thought, I went to Symmington's office. Megan might pay no attention to strictures on her conduct, but I would like to get things straight.

Mr Symmington was disengaged, I was told, and I was shown into his room. By a pinching of the lips, and an additional stiffness of manner, I gathered that I was not exactly popular at the moment.

'Good morning,' I said. 'I'm afraid this isn't a professional call, but a personal one. I'll put it plainly. I dare say you'll have realized that I'm in love with Megan. I've asked her to marry me and she has refused. But I'm not taking that as final.'

I saw Symmington's expression change, and I read his mind with ludicrous ease. Megan was a disharmonious element in his house. He was, I felt sure, a just and kindly man, and he would never have dreamed of not providing a home for his dead wife's daughter. But her marriage to me would certainly be a relief. The frozen halibut thawed. He gave me a pale cautious smile.

'Frankly, do you know, Burton, I had no idea of such a thing. I know you've taken a lot of notice of her, but we've always regarded her as such a child.'

'She's not a child,' I said shortly.

'No, no, not in years.'

'She can be her age any time she's allowed to be,' I said, still slightly angry. 'She's not twenty-one, I know, but she

will be in a month or two. I'll let you have all the information about myself you want. I'm well off and have led
quite a decent life. I'll look after her and do all I can to
make her happy.'

'Quite—quite. Still, it's up to Megan herself.'

'She'll come round in time,' I said. 'But I just thought
I'd like to get straight with you about it.'

He said he appreciated that, and we parted amicably.

I ran into Miss Emily Barton outside. She had a shopping
basket on her arm.

'Good morning, Mr Burton, I hear you went to London
yesterday.'

Yes, she had heard all right. Her eyes were, I thought,
kindly, but full of curiosity, too.

'I went to see my doctor,' I said.

Miss Emily smiled.

That smile made little of Marcus Kent. She murmured:

'I hear Megan nearly missed the train. She jumped in
when it was going.'

'Helped by me,' I said. 'I hauled her in.'

'How lucky you were there. Otherwise there might have
been an accident.'

It is extraordinary how much of a fool one gentle
inquisitive old maiden lady can make a man feel!

I was saved further suffering by the onslaught of
Mrs Dane Calthrop. She had her own tame elderly maiden
lady in tow, but she herself was full of direct speech.

'Good morning,' she said. 'I heard you've made Megan

buy herself some decent clothes? Very sensible of you. It takes a man to think of something really practical like that. I've been worried about that girl for a long time. Girls with brains are so liable to turn into morons, aren't they?'

With which remarkable statement, she shot into the fish shop.

Miss Marple, left standing by me, twinkled a little and said:

'Mrs Dane Calthrop is a very remarkable woman, you know. She's nearly always right.'

'It makes her rather alarming,' I said.

'Sincerity has that effect,' said Miss Marple.

Mrs Dane Calthrop shot out of the fish shop again and rejoined us. She was holding a large red lobster.

'Have you ever seen anything so unlike Mr Pye?' she said—'very virile and handsome, isn't it?'

I was a little nervous of meeting Joanna but I found when I got home that I needn't have worried. She was out and she did not return for lunch. This aggrieved Partridge a good deal, who said sourly as she proffered two loin chops in an entrée dish: 'Miss Burton said specially as she was going to be *in*.'

I ate both chops in an attempt to atone for Joanna's lapse. All the same, I wondered where my sister was. She had taken to be very mysterious about her doings of late.

It was half-past three when Joanna burst into the drawing-room. I had heard a car stop outside and I half expected to see Griffith, but the car drove on and Joanna came in alone.

Her face was very red and she seemed upset. I perceived that something had happened.

'What's the matter?' I asked.

Joanna opened her mouth, closed it again, sighed, plumped herself down in a chair and stared in front of her. She said:

'I've had the most awful day.'

'What's happened?'

'I've done the most incredible thing. It was awful—'

'But what—'

'I just started out for a walk, an ordinary walk—I went up over the hill and on to the moor. I walked miles—I felt like it. Then I dropped down into a hollow. There's a farm there—A God-forsaken lonely sort of spot. I was thirsty and I wondered if they'd got any milk or something. So I wandered into the farmyard and then the door opened and Owen came out.'

'Yes?'

'He thought it might be the district nurse. There was a woman in there having a baby. He was expecting the nurse and he'd sent word to her to get hold of another doctor. It—things were going wrong.'

'Yes?'

'So he said—to *me*. "Come on, you'll do—better than nobody." I said I couldn't, and he said what did I mean? I said I'd never done anything like that, that I didn't know anything—

'He said what the hell did that matter? And then he was

awful. He turned on me. He said, "You're a woman, aren't you? I suppose you can do your durnedest to help another woman?" And he went on at me—said I'd talked as though I was interested in doctoring and had said I wished I was a nurse. "All pretty talk, I suppose! You didn't mean anything real by it, but this *is* real and you're going to behave like a decent human being and not like a useless ornamental nit-wit!"

'I've done the most incredible things, Jerry. Held instruments and boiled them and handed things. I'm so tired I can hardly stand up. It was dreadful. But he saved her—and the baby. It was born alive. He didn't think at one time he could save it. Oh dear!'

Joanna covered her face with her hands.

I contemplated her with a certain amount of pleasure and mentally took my hat off to Owen Griffith. He'd brought Joanna slap up against reality for once.

I said, 'There's a letter for you in the hall. From Paul, I think.'

'Eh?' She paused for a minute and then said, 'I'd no idea, Jerry, what doctors had to *do*. The nerve they've got to have!'

I went out into the hall and brought Joanna her letter. She opened it, glanced vaguely at its contents, and let it drop.

'He was—really—rather wonderful. The way he fought— the way he wouldn't be beaten! He was rude and horrible to *me*—but he *was* wonderful.'

I observed Paul's disregarded letter with some pleasure. Plainly, Joanna was cured of Paul.

CHAPTER 13

Things never come when they are expected.

I was full of Joanna's and my personal affairs and was quite taken aback the next morning when Nash's voice said over the telephone: '*We've got her*, Mr Burton!'

I was so startled I nearly dropped the receiver.

'You mean the—'

He interrupted.

'Can you be overheard where you are?'

'No, I don't think so—well, perhaps—'

It seemed to me that the baize door to the kitchen had swung open a trifle.

'Perhaps you'd care to come down to the station?'

'I will. Right away.'

I was at the police station in next to no time. In an inner room Nash and Sergeant Parkins were together. Nash was wreathed in smiles.

'It's been a long chase,' he said. 'But we're there at last.'

He flicked a letter across the table. This time it was all typewritten. It was, of its kind, fairly mild.

'It's no use thinking you're going to step into a dead
woman's shoes. The whole town is laughing at you. Get
out now. Soon it will be too late. This is a warning.
Remember what happened to that other girl. Get out
and stay out.'

It finished with some mildly obscene language.

'That reached Miss Holland this morning,' said Nash.

'Thought it was funny she hadn't had one before,' said
Sergeant Parkins.

'Who wrote it?' I asked.

Some of the exultation faded out of Nash's face.

He looked tired and concerned. He said soberly:

'I'm sorry about it, because it will hit a decent man
hard, but there it is. Perhaps he's had his suspicions
already.'

'Who wrote it?' I reiterated.

'Miss Aimée Griffith.'

Nash and Parkins went to the Griffiths' house that afternoon with a warrant.

By Nash's invitation I went with them.

'The doctor,' he said, 'is very fond of you. He hasn't
many friends in this place. I think if it is not too painful
to you, Mr Burton, that you might help him to bear up
under the shock.'

I said I would come. I didn't relish the job, but I thought
I might be some good.

We rang the bell and asked for Miss Griffith and we

were shown into the drawing-room. Elsie Holland, Megan and Symmington were there having tea.

Nash behaved very circumspectly.

He asked Aimée if he might have a few words with her privately.

She got up and came towards us. I thought I saw just a faint hunted look in her eye. If so, it went again. She was perfectly normal and hearty.

'Want me? Not in trouble over my car lights again, I hope?'

She led the way out of the drawing-room and across the hall into a small study.

As I closed the drawing-room door, I saw Symmington's head jerk up sharply. I supposed his legal training had brought him in contact with police cases, and he had recognized something in Nash's manner. He half rose.

That is all I saw before I shut the door and followed the others.

Nash was saying his piece. He was very quiet and correct. He cautioned her and then told her that he must ask her to accompany him. He had a warrant for her arrest and he read out the charge—

I forget now the exact legal term. It was the letters, not murder yet.

Aimée Griffith flung up her head and bayed with laughter. She boomed out: 'What ridiculous nonsense! As though I'd write a packet of indecent stuff like that. You must be mad. I've never written a word of the kind.'

Nash had produced the letter to Elsie Holland. He said: 'Do you deny having written this, Miss Griffith?'

If she hesitated it was only for a split second.

'Of course I do. I've never seen it before.'

Nash said quietly: 'I must tell you, Miss Griffith, that you were observed to type that letter on the machine at the Women's Institute between eleven and eleven-thirty p.m. on the night before last. Yesterday you entered the post office with a bunch of letters in your hand—'

'I never posted this.'

'No, *you* did not. Whilst waiting for stamps, you dropped it inconspicuously on the floor, so that somebody should come along unsuspectingly and pick it up and post it.'

'I never—'

The door opened and Symmington came in. He said sharply: 'What's going on? Aimée, if there is anything wrong, you ought to be legally represented. If you wish me—'

She broke then. Covered her face with her hands and staggered to a chair. She said:

'Go away, Dick, go away. Not you! Not *you*!'

'You need a solicitor, my dear girl.'

'Not you. I—I—couldn't bear it. I don't want you to know—all this.'

He understood then, perhaps. He said quietly:

'I'll get hold of Mildmay, of Exhampton. Will that do?'

She nodded. She was sobbing now.

Symmington went out of the room. In the doorway he collided with Owen Griffith.

'What's this?' said Owen violently. 'My sister—'

'I'm sorry, Dr Griffith. Very sorry. But we have no alternative.'

'You think she—was responsible for those letters?'

'I'm afraid there is no doubt of it, sir,' said Nash—he turned to Aimée, 'You must come with us now, please, Miss Griffith—you shall have every facility for seeing a solicitor, you know.'

Owen cried: 'Aimée?'

She brushed past him without looking at him.

She said: 'Don't talk to me. Don't say anything. And for God's sake don't *look* at me!'

They went out. Owen stood like a man in a trance.

I waited a bit, then I came up to him.

'If there's anything I can do, Griffith, tell me.'

He said like a man in a dream:

'Aimée? I don't believe it.'

'It may be a mistake,' I suggested feebly.

He said slowly: 'She wouldn't take it like that if it were. But I would never have believed it. I *can't* believe it.'

He sank down on a chair. I made myself useful by finding a stiff drink and bringing it to him. He swallowed it down and it seemed to do him good.

He said: 'I couldn't take it in at first. I'm all right now. Thanks, Burton, but there's nothing you can do. Nothing *anyone* can do.'

The door opened and Joanna came in. She was very white.

She came over to Owen and looked at me.

She said: 'Get out, Jerry. This is my business.'

As I went out of the door, I saw her kneel down by his chair.

*

I can't tell you coherently the events of the next twenty-four hours. Various incidents stand out, unrelated to other incidents.

I remember Joanna coming home, very white and drawn, and of how I tried to cheer her up, saying:

'Now who's being a ministering angel?'

And of how she smiled in a pitiful twisted way and said:

'He says he won't have me, Jerry. He's very, *very* proud and stiff!'

And I said: 'My girl won't have me, either . . .'

We sat there for a while, Joanna saying at last:

'The Burton family isn't exactly in demand at the moment!'

I said, 'Never mind, my sweet, we still have each other,' and Joanna said, 'Somehow or other, Jerry, that doesn't comfort me much just now . . .'

Owen came the next day and rhapsodised in the most fulsome way about Joanna. She was wonderful, marvellous! The way she'd come to him, the way she was willing to marry him—at once if he liked. But he wasn't going to let her do that. No, she was too good, too fine to be associated with the kind of muck that would start as soon as the papers got hold of the news.

I was fond of Joanna, and knew she was the kind who's all right when standing by in trouble, but I got rather bored with all this high-falutin' stuff. I told Owen rather irritably not to be so damned noble.

I went down to the High Street and found everybody's

tongues wagging nineteen to the dozen. Emily Barton was saying that she had never really trusted Aimée Griffith. The grocer's wife was saying with gusto that she'd always thought Miss Griffith had a queer look in her eye—

They had completed the case against Aimée, so I learnt from Nash. A search of the house had brought to light the cut pages of Emily Barton's book—in the cupboard under the stairs, of all places, wrapped up in an old roll of wallpaper.

'And a jolly good place too,' said Nash appreciatively. 'You never know when a prying servant won't tamper with a desk or a locked drawer—but those junk cupboards full of last year's tennis balls and old wallpaper are never opened except to shove something more in.'

'The lady would seem to have had a *penchant* for that particular hiding-place,' I said.

'Yes. The criminal mind seldom has much variety. By the way, talking of the dead girl, we've got one fact to go upon. There's a large heavy pestle missing from the doctor's dispensary. I'll bet anything you like that's what she was stunned with.'

'Rather an awkward thing to carry about,' I objected.

'Not for Miss Griffith. She was going to the Guides that afternoon, but she was going to leave flowers and vegetables at the Red Cross stall on the way, so she'd got a whopping great basket with her.'

'You haven't found the skewer?'

'No, and I shan't. The poor devil may be mad, but she wasn't mad enough to keep a blood-stained skewer just to make it easy for us, when all she'd got to do was to wash it and return it to a kitchen drawer.'

'I suppose,' I conceded, 'that you can't have everything.'

The vicarage had been one of the last places to hear the news. Old Miss Marple was very much distressed by it. She spoke to me very earnestly on the subject.

'It isn't *true*, Mr Burton. I'm sure it isn't true.'

'It's true enough, I'm afraid. They were lying in wait, you know. They actually *saw* her type that letter.'

'Yes, yes—perhaps they did. Yes, I can understand *that*.'

'And the printed pages from which the letters were cut were found where she'd hidden them in her house.'

Miss Marple stared at me. Then she said, in a very low voice: 'But that is horrible—really *wicked*.'

Mrs Dane Calthrop came up with a rush and joined us and said: 'What's the matter, Jane?'

Miss Marple was murmuring helplessly:

'Oh dear, oh dear, what can one *do*?'

'What's upset you, Jane?'

Miss Marple said: 'There must be *something*. But I am so old and so ignorant, and I am afraid, so foolish.'

I felt rather embarrassed and was glad when Mrs Dane Calthrop took her friend away.

I was to see Miss Marple again that afternoon, however. Much later when I was on my way home.

She was standing near the little bridge at the end of the village, near Mrs Cleat's cottage, and talking to Megan of all people.

I wanted to see Megan. I had been wanting to see her all day. I quickened my pace. But as I came up to them, Megan turned on her heel and went off in the other direction.

It made me angry and I would have followed her, but Miss Marple blocked my way.

She said: 'I wanted to speak to you. No, don't go after Megan now. It wouldn't be wise.'

I was just going to make a sharp rejoinder when she disarmed me by saying:

'That girl has great courage—a very high order of courage.'

I still wanted to go after Megan, but Miss Marple said:

'Don't try and see her now. I do know what I am talking about. She must keep her courage intact.'

There was something about the old lady's assertion that chilled me. It was as though she knew something that I didn't.

I was afraid and didn't know why I was afraid.

I didn't go home. I went back into the High Street and walked up and down aimlessly. I don't know what I was waiting for, nor what I was thinking about . . .

I got caught by that awful old bore Colonel Appleton. He asked after my pretty sister as usual and then went on:

'What's all this about Griffith's sister being mad as a hatter? They say she's been at the bottom of this anonymous letter business that's been such a confounded nuisance to everybody? Couldn't believe it at first, but they say it's quite true.'

I said it was true enough.

'Well, well—I must say our police force is pretty good on the whole. Give 'em time, that's all, give 'em time. Funny business this anonymous letter stunt—these desiccated old maids are always the ones who go in for it—though the

Griffith woman wasn't bad looking even if she was a bit long in the tooth. But there aren't any decent-looking girls in this part of the world—except that governess girl of the Symmingtons. She's worth looking at. Pleasant girl, too. Grateful if one does any little thing for her. Came across her having a picnic or something with those kids not long ago. They were romping about in the heather and she was knitting—ever so vexed she'd run out of wool. "Well," I said, "like me to run you into Lymstock? I've got to call for a rod of mine there. I shan't be more than ten minutes getting it, then I'll run you back again." She was a bit doubtful about leaving the boys. "They'll be all right," I said. "Who's to harm them?" Wasn't going to have the boys along, no fear! So I ran her in, dropped her at the wool shop, picked her up again later and that was that. Thanked me very prettily. Grateful and all that. Nice girl.'

I managed to get away from him.

It was after that, that I caught sight of Miss Marple for the third time. She was coming out of the police station.

Where do one's fears come from? Where do they shape themselves? Where do they hide before coming out into the open?

Just one short phrase. Heard and noted and never quite put aside:

'Take me away—it's so awful being here—feeling so wicked . . .'

Why had Megan said that? What had she to feel wicked about?

214

There could be nothing in Mrs Symmington's death to make Megan feel wicked.

Why had the child felt wicked? Why? Why?

Could it be because she felt responsible in any way?

Megan? Impossible! *Megan* couldn't have had anything to do with those letters—those foul obscene letters.

Owen Griffith had known a case up North—a schoolgirl . . .

What had Inspector Graves said?

Something about an *adolescent mind . . .*

Innocent middle-aged ladies on operating tables babbling words they hardly knew. Little boys chalking up things on walls.

No, no, not *Megan*.

Heredity? Bad blood? An unconscious inheritance of something abnormal? Her misfortune, not her fault, a curse laid upon her by a past generation?

'I'm not the wife for you. I'm better at hating than loving.'

Oh, my Megan, my little child. Not *that*! Anything but that. And that old Tabby is after you, she suspects. She says you have courage. Courage to do *what*?

It was only a brainstorm. It passed. But I wanted to see Megan—I wanted to see her badly.

At half-past nine that night I left the house and went down to the town and along to the Symmingtons'.

It was then that an entirely new idea came into my mind. The idea of a woman whom nobody had considered for a moment.

(Or had Nash considered her?)

Wildly unlikely, wildly improbable, and I would have

215

said up to today impossible, too. But that was not so. No, not *impossible*.

I redoubled my pace. Because it was now even more imperative that I should see Megan straightaway.

I passed through the Symmingtons' gate and up to the house. It was a dark overcast night. A little rain was beginning to fall. The visibility was bad.

I saw a line of light from one of the windows. The little morning-room?

I hesitated a moment or two, then instead of going up to the front door, I swerved and crept very quietly up to the window, skirting a big bush and keeping low.

The light came from a chink in the curtains which were not quite drawn. It was easy to look through and see.

It was a strangely peaceful and domestic scene. Symmington in a big armchair, and Elsie Holland, her head bent, busily patching a boy's torn shirt.

I could hear as well as see for the window was open at the top.

Elsie Holland was speaking.

'But I do think, really, Mr Symmington, that the boys are quite old enough to go to boarding school. Not that I shan't hate leaving them because I shall. I'm ever so fond of them both.'

Symmington said: 'I think perhaps you're right about Brian, Miss Holland. I've decided that he shall start next term at Winhays—my old prep school. But Colin is a little young yet. I'd prefer him to wait another year.'

'Well of course I see what you mean. And Colin is perhaps a little young for his age—'

216

Quiet domestic talk—quiet domestic scene—and a golden head bent over needlework.

Then the door opened and Megan came in.

She stood very straight in the doorway, and I was aware at once of something tense and strung up about her. The skin of her face was tight and drawn and her eyes were bright and resolute. There was no diffidence about her tonight and no childishness.

She said, addressing Symmington, but giving him no title (and I suddenly reflected that I never heard her call him anything. Did she address him as father or as Dick or what?)

'I would like to speak to you, please. Alone.'

Symmington looked surprised and, I fancied, not best pleased. He frowned, but Megan carried her point with a determination unusual in her.

She turned to Elsie Holland and said:

'Do you mind, Elsie?'

'Oh, of course not,' Elsie Holland jumped up. She looked startled and a little flurried.

She went to the door and Megan came farther in so that Elsie passed her.

Just for a moment Elsie stood motionless in the doorway looking over her shoulder.

Her lips were closed, she stood quite still, one hand stretched out, the other clasping her needlework to her.

I caught my breath, overwhelmed by her beauty.

When I think of her now, I always think of her like that—in arrested motion, with that matchless deathless perfection that belonged to ancient Greece.

Then she went out shutting the door.

Symmington said rather fretfully:

'Well, Megan, what is it? What do you want?'

Megan had come right up to the table. She stood there looking down at Symmington. I was struck anew by the resolute determination of her face and by something else—a hardness new to me.

Then she opened her lips and said something that startled me to the core.

'I want some money,' she said.

The request didn't improve Symmington's temper. He said sharply:

'Couldn't you have waited until tomorrow morning? What's the matter, do you think your allowance is inadequate?'

A fair man, I thought even then, open to reason, though not to emotional appeal.

Megan said: 'I want a good deal of money.'

Symmington sat up straight in his chair. He said coldly:

'You will come of age in a few months' time. Then the money left you by your grandmother will be turned over to you by the public trustee.'

Megan said:

'You don't understand. I want money from *you*.' She went on, speaking faster. 'Nobody's ever talked much to me about my father. They've not wanted me to know about him. But I do know that he went to prison and I know why. It was for blackmail!'

She paused.

'Well, I'm his daughter. And perhaps I take after him.

Anyway, I'm asking you to give me money because—if you don't'—she stopped and then went on very slowly and evenly—'if you don't—*I shall say what I saw you doing to the cachet that day in my mother's room.*'

There was a pause. Then Symmington said in a completely emotionless voice:

'I don't know what you mean.'

Megan said: 'I think you do.'

And she smiled. It was not a nice smile.

Symmington got up. He went over to the writing desk. He took a cheque-book from his pocket and wrote out a cheque. He blotted it carefully and then came back. He held it out to Megan.

'You're grown up now,' he said. 'I can understand that you may feel you want to buy something rather special in the way of clothes and all that. I don't know what you're talking about. I didn't pay attention. But here's a cheque.'

Megan looked at it, then she said:

'Thank you. That will do to go on with.'

She turned and went out of the room. Symmington stared after her and at the closed door, then he turned round and as I saw his face I made a quick uncontrolled movement forward.

It was checked in the most extraordinary fashion. The big bush that I had noticed by the wall stopped being a bush. Superintendent Nash's arms went round me and Superintendent Nash's voice just breathed in my ear:

'Quiet, Burton. For God's sake.'

Then, with infinite caution he beat a retreat, his arm impelling me to accompany him.

Round the side of the house he straightened himself and wiped his forehead.

'Of course,' he said, 'you *would* have to butt in!'

'That girl isn't safe,' I said urgently. 'You saw his face? We've got to get her out of here.'

Nash took a firm grip of my arm.

'Now, look here, Mr Burton, you've got to *listen*.'

Well, I listened.

I didn't like it—but I gave in.

But I insisted on being on the spot and I swore to obey orders implicitly.

So that is how I came with Nash and Parkins into the house by the back door which was already unlocked.

And I waited with Nash on the upstairs landing behind the velvet curtain masking the window alcove until the clocks in the house struck two, and Symmington's door opened and he went across the landing and into Megan's room.

I did not stir or make a move for I knew that Sergeant Parkins was inside masked by the opening door, and I knew that Parkins was a good man and knew his job, and I knew that I couldn't have trusted myself to keep quiet and not break out.

And waiting there, with my heart thudding, I saw Symmington come out with Megan in his arms and carry her downstairs, with Nash and myself a discreet distance behind him.

He carried her through to the kitchen and he had just

arranged her comfortably with her head in the gas oven and had turned on the gas when Nash and I came through the kitchen door and switched on the light.

And that was the end of Richard Symmington. He collapsed. Even while I was hauling Megan out and turning off the gas I saw the collapse. He didn't even try to fight. He knew he'd played and lost.

Upstairs I sat by Megan's bed waiting for her to come round and occasionally cursing Nash.

'How do you know she's all right? It was too big a risk.'

Nash was very soothing.

'Just a soporific in the milk she always had by her bed. Nothing more. It stands to reason, he couldn't risk her being poisoned. As far as he's concerned the whole business is closed with Miss Griffith's arrest. He can't afford to have any mysterious death. No violence, no poison. But if a rather unhappy type of girl broods over her mother's suicide, and finally goes and puts her head in the gas oven—well, people just say that she was never quite normal and the shock of her mother's death finished her.'

I said, watching Megan:

'She's a long time coming round.'

'You heard what Dr Griffith said? Heart and pulse quite all right—she'll just sleep and wake naturally. Stuff he gives a lot of his patients, he says.'

Megan stirred. She murmured something.

Superintendent Nash unobtrusively left the room.

Presently Megan opened her eyes. 'Jerry.'

'Hallo, sweet.'

'Did I do it well?'

'You might have been blackmailing ever since your cradle!'

Megan closed her eyes again. Then she murmured:

'Last night—I was writing to you—in case anything went—went wrong. But I was too sleepy to finish. It's over there.'

I went across to the writing-table. In a shabby little blotter I found Megan's unfinished letter.

'My dear Jerry,' it began primly:

'I was reading my school Shakespeare and the sonnet that begins:

"So are you to my thoughts as food to life
  Or as sweet-season'd showers are to the ground."

and I see that I am in love with you after all, because that is what I feel . . .'

CHAPTER 14

'So you see,' said Mrs Dane Calthrop, 'I was quite right to call in an expert.'

I stared at her. We were all at the vicarage. The rain was pouring down outside and there was a pleasant log fire, and Mrs Dane Calthrop had just wandered round, beat up a sofa cushion and put it for some reason of her own on the top of the grand piano.

'But did you?' I said, surprised. 'Who was it? What did he do?'

'It wasn't a he,' said Mrs Dane Calthrop.

With a sweeping gesture she indicated Miss Marple. Miss Marple had finished the fleecy knitting and was now engaged with a crochet hook and a ball of cotton.

'That's my expert,' said Mrs Dane Calthrop. 'Jane Marple. Look at her well. I tell you, that woman knows more about the different kinds of human wickedness than anyone I've ever known.'

'I don't think you should put it quite like that, dear,' murmured Miss Marple.

'But you do.'

'One sees a good deal of human nature living in a village all the year round,' said Miss Marple placidly.

Then, seeming to feel it was expected of her, she laid down her crochet, and delivered a gentle old-maidish dissertation on murder.

'The great thing is in these cases to keep an absolutely open mind. Most crimes, you see, are so absurdly simple. This one was. Quite sane and straightforward—and quite understandable—in an unpleasant way, of course.'

'Very unpleasant!'

'The truth was really so very obvious. *You* saw it, you know, Mr Burton.'

'Indeed I did not.'

'But you did. You indicated the whole thing to me. You saw perfectly the relationship of one thing to the other, but you just hadn't enough self-confidence to see what those feelings of yours meant. To begin with, that tiresome phrase "No smoke without fire." It irritated you, but you proceeded quite correctly to label it for what it was—a smoke screen. Misdirection, you see—everybody looking at the wrong thing—the anonymous letters, but the whole point was that there *weren't* any anonymous letters!'

'But my dear Miss Marple, I can assure you that there *were*. I had one.'

'Oh yes, but they weren't real at all. Dear Maud here tumbled to that. Even in peaceful Lymstock there are plenty of scandals, and I can assure you any *woman* living in the place would have known about them and used them. But a man, you see, isn't interested in gossip in the same way—especially a detached logical man like Mr Symmington. A genuine woman writer of those letters would have made her letters much more to the point.

'So you see that if you disregard the smoke and come to the fire you know where you are. You just come down to the actual facts of what happened. And putting aside the letters, just one thing happened—Mrs Symmington died.

'So then, naturally, one thinks of who might have wanted Mrs Symmington to die, and of course the very first person one thinks of in such a case is, I am afraid, the *husband*. And one asks oneself is there any *reason*?—any *motive*?—for instance, *another* woman?

'And the very first thing I hear is that there is a very attractive young governess in the house. So clear, isn't it? Mr Symmington, a rather dry repressed unemotional man, tied to a querulous and neurotic wife and then suddenly this radiant young creature comes along.

'I'm afraid, you know, that gentlemen, when they fall in love at a certain age, get the disease very badly. It's quite a madness. And Mr Symmington, as far as I can make out, was never actually a *good* man—he wasn't very kind or very affectionate or very sympathetic—his qualities were all negative—so he hadn't really the strength to fight his madness. And in a place like this, only his wife's death would solve his problem. He wanted to marry the girl, you see. She's very respectable and so is he. And besides, he's devoted to his children and didn't want to give them up. He wanted everything, his home, his children, his respectability and Elsie. And the price he would have to pay for that was murder.

'He chose, I do think, a very clever way. He knew so well from his experience of criminal cases how soon suspicion falls on the husband if a wife dies unexpectedly—and the possibility of exhumation in the case of poison. So he created a death which seemed only incidental to something else. He created a non-existent anonymous letter writer. And the clever thing was that the police were certain to suspect a *woman*—and they were quite right in a way. All the letters *were* a woman's letters; he cribbed them very cleverly from the letters in the case last year and from a case Dr Griffith told him about. I don't mean that he was so crude as to reproduce any letter verbatim, but he took phrases and expressions from them and mixed them up, and the net result was that the letters definitely represented a woman's mind—a half-crazed repressed personality.

'He knew all the tricks that the police use, handwriting, typewriting tests, etc. He's been preparing his crime for some time. He typed all the envelopes before he gave away the typewriter to the Women's Institute, and he cut the pages from the book at Little Furze probably quite a long time ago when he was waiting in the drawing-room one day. People don't open books of sermons much!

'And finally, having got his false Poison Pen well established, he staged the real thing. A fine afternoon when the governess and the boys and his step-daughter would be out, and the servants having their regular day out. He couldn't foresee that the little maid Agnes would quarrel with her boy and come back to the house.'

Joanna asked:

'But what did she *see*? Do you know that?'

'I don't *know*. I can only guess. My guess would be that she didn't see anything.'

'That it was all a mare's nest?'

'No, no, my dear, I mean that she stood at the pantry window all the afternoon waiting for the young man to come and make it up and that—quite literally—she saw *nothing*. That is, *no one* came to the house at all, not the postman, nor anybody else.

'It would take her some time, being slow, to realize that that was very odd—because apparently Mrs Symmington *had* received an anonymous letter that afternoon.'

'Didn't she receive one?' I asked, puzzled.

'But of course not! As I say, this crime is so simple. Her husband just put the cyanide in the top cachet of the ones she took in the afternoon when her sciatica came on after lunch. All Symmington had to do was to get home before, or at the same time as Elsie Holland, call his wife, get no answer, go up to her room, drop a spot of cyanide in the plain glass of water she had used to swallow the cachet, toss the crumpled-up anonymous letter into the grate, and put by her hand the scrap of paper with "*I can't go on*" written on it.'

Miss Marple turned to me.

'You were quite right about that, too, Mr Burton. A "scrap of paper" was all wrong. People don't leave suicide notes on small torn scraps of paper. They use a *sheet* of paper—and very often an envelope too. Yes, the scrap of paper was wrong and you knew it.'

'You are rating me too high,' I said. 'I knew nothing.'

'But you did, you really *did*, Mr Burton. Otherwise why were you immediately impressed by the message your sister left scribbled on the telephone pad?'

I repeated slowly, '"Say that *I can't go on* Friday"—I see! *I can't go on?*'

Miss Marple beamed on me.

'Exactly. Mr Symmington came across such a message and saw its possibilities. He tore off the words he wanted for when the time came—a message genuinely in his wife's handwriting.'

'Was there any further brilliance on my part?' I asked.

Miss Marple twinkled at me.

'You put me on the track, you know. You assembled those facts together for me—in sequence—and on top of it you told me the most important thing of all—that Elsie Holland had never received any anonymous letters.'

'Do you know,' I said, 'last night I thought that *she* was the letter writer and that that was why there had been no letters written to her?'

'Oh dear, me, no . . . The person who writes anonymous letters practically always sends them to herself as well. That's part of the—well, the excitement, I suppose. No, no, the fact interested me for *quite* another reason. It was really, you see, Mr Symmington's one weakness. He couldn't bring himself to write a foul letter to the girl he loved. It's a very interesting sidelight on human nature—and a credit to him, in a way—but it's where he gave himself away.'

Joanna said:

'And he killed Agnes? But surely that was quite unnecessary?'

'Perhaps it was, but what you don't realize, my dear (not having killed any one), is that your judgment is distorted afterwards and everything seems exaggerated.

228

No doubt he heard the girl telephoning to Partridge, saying she'd been worried ever since Mrs Symmington's death, that there was something she didn't understand. He can't take any chances—this stupid, foolish girl has seen *something*, knows something.'

'Yet apparently he was at his office all that afternoon?'

'I should imagine he killed her before he went. Miss Holland was in the dining-room and kitchen. He just went out into the hall, opened and shut the front door as though he had gone out, then slipped into the little cloakroom. When only Agnes was left in the house, he probably rang the front-door bell, slipped back into the cloakroom, came out behind her and hit her on the head as she was opening the front door, and then after thrusting the body into the cupboard, he hurried along to his office, arriving just a little late if anyone had happened to notice it, but they probably didn't. You see, no one was suspecting a *man*.'

'Abominable brute,' said Mrs Dane Calthrop.

'You're not sorry for him, Mrs Dane Calthrop?' I inquired.

'Not in the least. Why?'

'I'm glad to hear it, that's all.'

Joanna said:

'But why Aimée Griffith? I know that the police have found the pestle taken from Owen's dispensary—and the skewer too. I suppose it's not so easy for a man to return things to kitchen drawers. And guess where they were? Superintendent Nash only told me just now when I met him on my way here. In one of those musty old deed-boxes in his office. Estate of Sir Jasper Harrington-West, deceased.'

229

'Poor Jasper,' said Mrs Dane Calthrop. 'He was a cousin of mine. Such a correct old boy. He would have had a fit!'

'Wasn't it madness to keep them?' I asked.

'Probably madder to throw them away,' said Mrs Dane Calthrop. 'No one had any suspicions about Symington.'

'He didn't strike her with the pestle,' said Joanna. 'There was a clock weight there too, with hair and blood on it. He pinched the pestle, they think, on the day Aimée was arrested, and hid the book pages in her house. And that brings me back to my original question. What about Aimée Griffith? The police actually *saw* her write that letter.'

'Yes, of course,' said Miss Marple. 'She did write *that* letter.'

'But why?'

'Oh, my dear, surely you have realized that Miss Griffith had been in love with Symington all her life?'

'Poor thing!' said Mrs Dane Calthrop mechanically.

'They'd always been good friends, and I dare say she thought, after Mrs Symington's death, that some day, perhaps—well—' Miss Marple coughed delicately. 'And then the gossip began spreading about Elsie Holland and I expect that upset her badly. She thought of the girl as a designing minx worming her way into Symington's affections and quite unworthy of him. And so, I think, she succumbed to temptation. Why not add one more anonymous letter, and frighten the girl out of the place? It must have seemed quite safe to her and she took, as she thought, every precaution.'

'Well?' said Joanna. 'Finish the story.'

'I should imagine,' said Miss Marple slowly, 'that when Miss Holland showed that letter to Symington he realized at once who had written it, and he saw a chance to finish the case once and for all, and make himself safe. Not very nice—no, not very nice, but he was frightened, you see. The police wouldn't be satisfied until they'd got the anonymous letter writer. When he took the letter down to the police and he found they'd actually seen Aimée writing it, he felt he'd got a chance in a thousand of finishing the whole thing.

'He took the family to tea there that afternoon and as he came from the office with his attaché case, he could easily bring the torn-out book pages to hide under the stairs and clinch the case. Hiding them under the stairs was a neat touch. It recalled the disposal of Agnes's body, and, from the practical point of view, it was very easy for him. When he followed Aimée and the police, just a minute or two in the hall passing through would be enough.'

'All the same,' I said, 'there's one thing I can't forgive you for, Miss Marple—roping in Megan.'

Miss Marple put down her crochet which she had resumed. She looked at me over her spectacles and her eyes were stern.

'My dear young man, *something* had to be done. There was no evidence against this very clever and unscrupulous man. I needed someone to help me, someone of high courage and good brains. I found the person I needed.'

'It was very dangerous for her.'

'Yes, it was dangerous, but we are not put into this world, Mr Burton, to avoid danger when an innocent fellow-creature's life is at stake. You understand me?'

I understood.

CHAPTER 15

Morning in the High Street.

Miss Emily Barton comes out of the grocer's with her shopping bag. Her cheeks are pink and her eyes are excited.

'Oh, dear, Mr Burton, I really am in such a flutter. To think I really am going on a cruise at last!'

'I hope you'll enjoy it.'

'Oh, I'm sure I shall. I should never have dared to go by myself. It does seem so *providential* the way everything has turned out. For a long time I've felt that I ought to part with Little Furze, that my means were really *too* straitened but I couldn't bear the idea of *strangers* there. But now that you have bought it and are going to live there with Megan— it is quite different. And then dear Aimée, after her terrible ordeal, not quite knowing what to do with herself, and her brother getting married (how nice to think you have *both* settled down with us!) and agreeing to come with me. We mean to be away quite a long time. We might even'—Miss Emily dropped her voice—'*go round the world*! And Aimée is so splendid and so practical. I really do think, don't you, that everything turns out for the *best*?'

Just for a fleeting moment I thought of Mrs Symmington and Agnes Woddell in their graves in the churchyard and wondered if they would agree, and then I remembered that Agnes's boy hadn't been very fond of her and that Mrs Symmington hadn't been very nice to Megan and, what the hell? we've all got to die some time! And I agreed with happy Miss Emily that everything was for the best in the best of possible worlds.

I went along the High Street and in at the Symmingtons' gate and Megan came out to meet me.

It was not a romantic meeting because an out-size Old English sheepdog came out with Megan and nearly knocked me over with his ill-timed exuberance.

'Isn't he *adorable*?' said Megan.

'A little overwhelming. Is he ours?'

'Yes, he's a wedding present from Joanna. We *have* had nice wedding presents, haven't we? That fluffy woolly thing that we don't know what it's for from Miss Marple, and the lovely Crown Derby tea-set from Mr Pye, and Elsie has sent me a toast-rack—'

'How typical,' I interjected.

'And she's got a post with a dentist and is very happy. And—where was I?'

'Enumerating wedding presents. Don't forget if you change your mind you'll have to send them all back.'

'I shan't change my mind. What else have we got? Oh, yes, Mrs Dane Calthrop has sent an Egyptian scarab.'

'Original woman,' I said.

'Oh! Oh! but you don't know the best. *Partridge* has actually sent me a present. It's the most hideous teacloth you've ever seen. But I think she *must* like me now because she says she embroidered it all with her own hands.'

'In a design of sour grapes and thistles, I suppose?'

'No, true lovers' knots.'

'Dear, dear,' I said, 'Partridge *is* coming on.'

Megan had dragged me into the house.

She said:

'There's just one thing I can't make out. Besides the dog's own collar and lead, Joanna has sent an extra collar and lead. What do you think that's for?'

'That,' I said, 'is Joanna's little joke.'